Also by Paul Mosier

Train I Ride

Echo's Sister

SUMMER and JULY

PAUL MOSIER

HARPER
An Imprint of HarperCollinsPublishers

Library of Congress Cataloging-in-Publication Data

Names: Mosier, Paul, author.
Title: Summer and July / Paul Mosier.
Description: First edition. | New York, NY : Harper, an imprint of
   HarperCollinsPublishers, [2020] | Audience: Ages 8-12. | Audience:
   Grades 4-6. |
Summary: When twelve-year-old goth girl Juillet and thirteen-year-old surfer
   girl Summer meet, they set aside their painful pasts and begin to transform
   into the people they would like to be. Identifiers: LCCN 2019028464 |
   ISBN 9780062849366 (hardcover)
Subjects: CYAC: Friendship—Fiction. | Self-actualization (Psychology)—
   Fiction. | Surfing—Fiction. | Mothers and daughters—Fiction. | Goth
   culture (Subculture)—Fiction. | Santa Monica (Calif.)—Fiction.
Classification: LCC PZ7.1.M6773 Sum 2020 | DDC [Fic]—dc23
LC record available at https://lccn.loc.gov/2019028464

Typography by Jessie Gang
20 21 22 23 24   PC/LSCH   10 9 8 7 6 5 4 3 2 1

First Edition

For Keri, Eleri, and Harmony,
and our days at the cottage by the sea

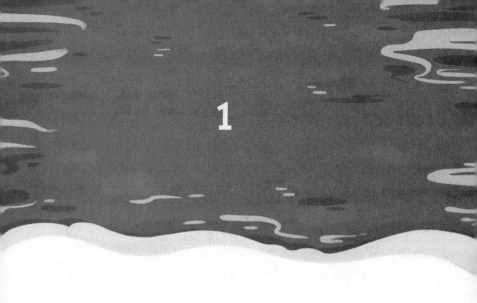

1

IT'S THE FIRST day of July in what will certainly be the most dreadful summer of my life. Day one of my month long confinement, to be spent in a neighborhood called Ocean Park, in a town called Santa Monica.

Mom says she visited tourist websites that claim this place is safe and walkable, filled with cute shops and cafés. But looking at the map, it's surrounded by crime-ridden Los Angeles on three sides and the shark-infested Pacific Ocean on the other.

The airplane hasn't even landed yet, and already this is the worst trip I've ever been on. To begin with, Mom and I had to wake up at the crack of dawn to catch the plane. Waking up early is bad enough during the school year, but it's just plain cruel in summer.

Because Mom wants me to start living more dangerously, instead of sitting in first class we're in coach, where the seats are narrow. I'm squeezed between Mom, who has the window seat, and an old man whose bony head is rolled up against my shoulder.

I nudge Mom with my elbow, and she looks up from the airline magazine she's been absorbed in.

"I think he's *dead*," I whisper urgently, gesturing with a nod to the old man on my shoulder.

Mom leans forward, looking past me to the cadaver I'm referring to, then smiles and goes back to her reading.

"Mom!" I whisper emphatically. "He hasn't even twitched for three states!"

I glance again at the old man, who cheerfully introduced himself as Walter before passing away shortly after takeoff. Now the only movement from him is his wispy hair blowing in the breeze of the overhead air circulators.

I'm a little on edge, because I'm not a fan of flying. I'm not a fan of falling to my death from thirty-five thousand feet, which I'm fairly sure is going to happen in spite of the soothing tones of the pilot's voice. He comes on the intercom every few minutes and tells us everything is fine, but he's probably freaking out up there in the cockpit. He isn't allowed to come on the

2

speaker and scream that the plane is going down.

I suffer from a variety of crippling fears, but Mom refuses to acknowledge or respect them. She insists they aren't real, that I'm making them up, just because she took me to five different psychologists and they all agreed with her. They all said I'm pretending to be afraid of things that according to them *cannot* actually harm me, because I don't want to think about something that *has* harmed me already. Namely my dad leaving Mom and me to run away with a fashion model. And even though Dad's leaving stinks and even though I hate him because of it, my fears are definitely real. I bet if *I* were paying the psychologists instead of my mom, they'd agree with *me* instead.

My most urgent fear up here at thirty-five thousand feet is the fear of gravity. Thanks to Sir Isaac Newton it's one of my worst fears, because pretty much everything wants to be closer to the center of the earth than it already is. Especially this airplane. It's just how gravity works.

Of course the flight attendants explained what we're supposed to do when this plane crashes. They went over it in great detail before we even took off. It's insane to talk about what to do when we fall from the sky, and then leave the ground anyway, and I'm the only person on the whole plane who paid attention to what the flight attendants were saying.

I'm also the only person who carefully studied the safety guide showing how to operate the oxygen masks, and where the emergency exits are. The cartoon people in the safety illustrations look like they're having a great time sliding off the wing on the inflatable yellow slide. Like they'll wanna climb back onto the wing for another turn. But none of the people on this plane look like the cartoon people in the safety guide, and none of the people sitting around me took the time to learn how to open the door or inflate the slide. If anyone gets off this plane alive, it'll be thanks to me, a twelve-year-old girl.

Finally the seat-belt light overhead lights up, and the ding thing goes *ding*, indicating it's time to die. But all the other passengers are oblivious. They still want to finish enjoying their continental breakfasts and coffees and cocktails before the flight attendants take their cups and napkins. I guess they might as well enjoy their last meal.

Below us is a blindingly bright mass of clouds reflecting the light of the sun. It's all happy up here above, and the clouds look cushiony soft below, but it's an illusion. We'll drop like a stone through the water vapor.

Now we sink into the clouds and we can't see a thing.

Nor can the pilot. We could hit a building or a wind turbine or another plane, or overshoot the runway and land in the ocean and be eaten by sharks. I clench my hands on the armrests and look at Mom, who gazes contentedly at an advertisement for a wax museum in the touristy airline magazine. The wax figures gaze contentedly back at her.

Suddenly we're below the clouds and the ground is close, a golf course and a freeway and then apartments and hotels, and parked airplanes, and a runway, which rudely greets the tires of our airplane with a horrendous scuffing noise.

Well. If one must obey the laws of gravity, I suppose the runway is the best place to do it.

I practically jump out of my seat when Walter, the dead guy, suddenly raises his head and turns to me. "Are we here already?"

I nod, reaching for the shoulder he used as a pillow for half a continent. I try to rub some feeling back into it.

The only downside to landing—instead of crashing or plunging into the sea—is the silent, smug satisfaction of my mom, who isn't afraid of any of these things. It's a victory for her that we didn't crash. She smiles pleasantly as she returns the in-flight magazine into the seat-back pocket. In spite of being an emergency-room doctor and having to witness all the things that can go wrong every day at her job—which she tells me about in horrifying detail on the few occasions I see her—she's blind to the dangers that surround us. It's like her brain was completely used up in medical school, so there's nothing left to tell her what she should be afraid of.

We plod down the weird little hallway that takes us from our plane to the airport. We wait at the carousel for our luggage. Then we head to the curb. The outside air is cool and breezy, and you can feel the ocean on it. But we are at an airport, not a beach, so cars and buses and taxis stream past. Finally an airport bus pulls up in front of us.

"This is us," Mom says.

"Aren't we taking a Lyft?"

She hauls her suitcases onto the little bus, and motions for me to follow.

"I've got it all planned out. We're taking this bus to the LAX City Bus Terminal, then the Santa Monica city bus to the neighborhood we're staying in."

"Why?" I practically trip on my bags as I drag them aboard.

"Because this is how people travel."

"I don't want to travel like people." The bus starts

moving and I almost fall down. "I like traveling like we used to."

Mom smiles at a bearded guy whose face is inches from hers. He looks bored.

"Well, this trip is going to give you some new experiences." She grips the overhead bar. "I grew up riding buses."

The airport bus takes forever, stopping at all the airport terminals and then a parking lot, and finally dumps us at the LAX City Bus Terminal. Next we jump on a big blue bus that's actually called the Big Blue Bus, where I sit next to smelly pickpockets, lepers, and lunatics while crushed beneath my suitcases. After several nauseating miles we finally get off on a sketchy corner, and lug our luggage on a sidewalk up a steep hill for a few grueling blocks. At last, Mom turns around from the top of the hill, a big smile on her face.

"Look!"

I drag my suitcase beside her and raise my eyes. Ahead of us, the land slopes downward for a few blocks of houses, past a street with businesses, then a narrow green park, beyond which are a strip of sand and the endless blue sea.

"Isn't it beautiful?" Mom beams.

"I'm too tired for beauty."

I didn't mean to sound so snarky and unenthusiastic. And really, it does look beautiful, like a hologram postcard. It's just that I'm exhausted, and I'm also mad at Mom that this month away from home ruined my plans of hanging out at the mall with Fern, looking at boys and eating soft pretzels with brown mustard.

We haul our suitcases half a block down a street called Fourth to a tall hedge, behind which is an old cottage that really could use a fresh coat of paint, and a front door with a rotting welcome mat. Under the mat is a key, which opens the door to a living room that causes Mom to gasp with desperate happiness. There's a big wooden table in what must be the dining room. Beyond that is the kitchen. I stand at the front door while Mom moves through the rooms. I watch as she opens up the cupboards and drawers.

"Look! It has everything we need. Plates and silverware and glasses. Spices. Condiments in the refrigerator. Even brown mustard!"

"We have all of that at home."

Mom turns to me. "This is gonna be fun. And it'll be good for you to get out of your comfort zone."

I frown. "Comfort is comfortable."

"How about we unpack and then go check out Main Street? Let's wear our swimsuits so we can test the water before the sun goes down!"

I shrug. Today is probably the last time I'll see her all month, as she'll be busy teaching interns in the ER at a nearby hospital, and attending a conference. That's pretty much the definition of our relationship. But she's acting like things are going to be different for the month we are in California. The hospital here is part of the same system as the one she works at back home, and she thinks it'll count as a vacation just because she'll ignore me while working in a seaside town. But if she can fake it for one day, maybe I can too.

Trying to salvage our relationship by avoiding me in a new setting is just one of the reasons Mom has dragged me here. She's also trying to *destroy* my friendship with Fern, who is pretty much the only person who supports me and my fears. Fern and I spend our time indoors at the mall, where things are predictable. Mom thinks I need to spend less time with Fern and more time doing things that could possibly kill me.

I drag my suitcases into the smaller bedroom with the single bed. The room has wood floors, as does the entire cottage, and windows on two sides with white curtains. I'm moving my folded clothes into the dresser drawers when I make a horrifying discovery—an aqua-colored one-piece swimsuit with a mermaid on the front.

"Mom!" My shout fills the cottage. "What is this mermaid abomination? And where is my skull-and-crossbones swimsuit?"

Mom appears in the doorway of my temporary bedroom. "I thought this one looked more beachy. It's cute, huh?"

One day. I can fake it for one day.

It's a good thing I brought all my makeup in my carry-on, or Mom would have tried to make me leave it back home, too. I like to wear black makeup and black clothes so I don't have to explain to Mom and everyone else that I'm not happy, and Mom is always trying to put me in sunny colors and make me look like I *am*.

After unpacking and resting, we walk down Main Street in the late afternoon. I keep my arms folded in front of me to hide as much of the mermaid swimsuit as possible. At least I'm wearing my black Converse high-tops with the skulls and crossbones I painted on the ankles with white nail polish.

Mom is acting all enchanted by the boutiques and restaurants. She's doing the slow-stroll thing that people do when they don't really have anywhere particular to go.

Main Street has a place to buy espresso every hundred feet. It also smells like pizza and dried pee and Mexican food and, above all, the sea. There's a toy shop that makes me wish I were eight instead of almost thirteen.

"This place looks cute," she says, stopping in front of an ice cream shop.

I scowl. "Pinkie Promise?" That's the name of the place. I'm not in the mood for anything cute.

Mom smiles. "Let's try it! We'll be here a whole month. We need to know where the good treats are, right?"

I shrug. Mom takes my hand and leads me inside.

I shake my hand loose from hers when I see the cute guy behind the counter, who looks like a surfer prince, with black skin and long blond hair that looks like it's never been brushed. I've never seen someone with black skin and blond hair before, but I've never been to California before, either. He's like what the football brutes and hockey jocks look like back home, but maybe a little more interesting. He's possibly old enough to be out of high school, so it's not like I'm trying to look all sophisticated and grown-up by shaking my hand loose from Mom's. It's just that I don't want to look like I can't walk by myself.

"Hello, ladies," he says, grinning. "How's the surf?"

"We don't surf," Mom says. "It's our first day here and we just put on our bathing suits to test the water."

Ugh. Mom doesn't understand that you're supposed to act like a local. Don't carry tourist guides, don't let anyone know you're lost. Anyway, she's not going to get me to even put my feet in the ocean. And this is absolutely the last time I'm wearing this mermaid bathing suit.

"Well, welcome to Ocean Park, *amigas!*" exclaims the surfer dude. "What sounds tasty today?"

"Hmm . . ." Mom leans over the case and looks inside. "Can I have a sample of the cherries jubilee?"

I roll my eyes. Mom also doesn't realize you aren't supposed to annoy the cute guy at the counter by asking for samples. The surfer dude dips a tiny pink spoon into the cherries jubilee and presents it to her. She tastes it, and gets this dreamy expression on her face, like she's remembering climbing cherry trees in her childhood or something.

"That's quite lovely. I'll have a cup of that."

"Excellent choice." Surfer dude scoops, delivers. "And how about you, young Betty?"

I frown a little. "My name isn't *Betty.*"

Someone laughs behind us. I turn for a quick glance and see a girl my age who looks like a movie star, with the sort of golden hair you only see on kindergarteners, or on the big screen. As gold as a gold crayon.

I turn back to the surfer dude, who's still waiting for my order. "Just a cup of pistachio, please."

"Comin' right up!"

As he reaches into the fluorescent-lit refrigerated case, I do another quick glance behind. The girl smiles, and I wonder why.

"Here you are, Betty." The surfer guy at the counter hands me my cup and spoon. "Otis, at your service." He does a little bow, with his hands held together like he's praying. "I'm here almost every day after my morning waves. I hope to see the two of you many times during your stay."

Mom takes her wallet out of her canvas beach bag. "How much do we owe you, Otis?"

He slaps his hand to his forehead. "Dude! I almost forgot."

Mom smiles and hands her debit card to Otis, who furrows his brow and looks at the register terminal.

"Stop flirting, Otis." It's the girl behind us. I do another quick turn. The girl smiles again.

I watch to make sure Mom remembers to tip. She gets her card back and we leave the register. Mom and I head toward the door, and the girl stares at me, like I must be the strangest thing she's ever seen.

"Hang loose!" Otis calls out as we leave.

Pinkie Promise is tiny, with no tables, so we eat on the sticky bench outside. The girl who laughed at me comes out with her cup of ice cream, mashing her face against the whipped cream on top like she's in a commercial for this place. She smiles again, and gives a little wave, then makes her way down the sidewalk, all beach-movie-like in her bathing suit and bare feet.

I look at my reflection in the store window, at my Goth makeup. Maybe it's a look the girl hasn't seen much of.

We go to the shore as the sun lowers toward the sea. Mom sets her bag on the sand and kicks her feet in the water. It's sad to watch. She thinks she's having fun, she calls me to join her. But I stay standing in my black high-tops, watching the waves. I could go into the water, maybe manage to enjoy myself. But then the waves would get bigger, and the tide would roll away suddenly, only to come roaring back in a giant wall of water that washes all this happiness away.

ON THE SECOND of July I wake up late. Mom left the windows of the little house open, and the white curtains blow into my temporary bedroom. It's like she doesn't even care if raccoons come in and maul me. Or if someone crawls in and takes me away. I can spend the rest of my childhood in a cult as far as she's concerned. They'll most likely brainwash me, and the next time Mom sees me I'll be selling friendship bracelets on a sidewalk somewhere, with my new sisters, while some guy in a van waits and counts the money.

I think about this and other likely outcomes from beneath the sheets, until thoughts of the sweet cereal in the cupboard get me out of bed. Mom only buys healthy cereals, but this cottage is stocked with the kinds of things kids like.

It's only nine o'clock here in California. It'd be noon back home in Michigan.

Mom went to the hospital before the sun came up. She won't be back here until the sun goes down. In the kitchen I see that she made coffee, which has turned to sludge. I pour a bowl of sugar-laminated flakes and sit in the front room eating them.

Mom has the Beach Boys playing surf music on internet radio. She's obviously trying to make me excited about a whole month where I'm within reach of sharks and tsunamis.

The summer morning passes through the open windows of the front room. The breezy white curtains make me feel like I'm in a commercial for laundry detergent.

Over the Beach Boys and the chirping of birds outside I hear the sound of a skateboard coming my way, the wheels hiccuping at every new section of sidewalk. *Da-duh, da-duh, da-duh.*

Then it stops. I hear a scratching noise, faintly, in the quiet between a song about a girl and a song about a wave. Then the skateboard noise again. *Da-duh, da-duh, da-duh,* back the direction it came from.

Then just the crunch of sugar-laminated breakfast flakes, the Beach Boys, my footsteps on the hardwood floors, the clink of my bowl set in the kitchen sink.

There's a note from Mom on the counter that I missed while pouring my cereal and milk.

Juillet—

Good morning! Happy first full day of your summer holiday! Here is a list of goals for your month in Ocean Park:

More exercise and fresh air.

Confront your fears.

Go outside your comfort zone!

I've left space for you to add to the list!

Also, please go to the grocery today and get the following:

Blueberries

Bread

Butter

Ground coffee, dark

Maybe a healthier choice of cereal?

Anything else that sounds good to you!

There's a healthy grocery store nearby, called Conscious Consumption. It's about a fifteen-minute walk. Reusable grocery bags are under the sink.

See map below, and attached cash. Keep the change for fun.

You're a smart, capable young woman. You can navigate this neighborhood and stay safe during the month we are here. It's time for me to be brave enough to let you prove it.

That said, please don't cross Lincoln, and stay between Rose Avenue and Colorado Avenue, which is where the pier is. The library is just a couple blocks away, and there is plenty to see on Main Street. And of course the beach!

Thank you, and enjoy!

Love, Mom

PS. Keep your phone with you so I can track where you are!

Attached with a paper clip is a hundred-dollar bill, which eases my dread only slightly. My hope was to not leave this house the entire month, but it looks like that's not going to last the first full day. Mom's crazy idea is that being in a strange place without my only friend for thirty-one days will somehow be fun and adventurous.

I tear off the top part of the note—the part with Mom's goals for me—and crumple it up and throw it in the wastebasket beneath the sink. She should make some goals for herself instead, like possibly spending time with her daughter every now and then.

In my room I pull on my jeans, my big toes getting caught in the rips in the legs once on the left and twice on the right. Next I deck myself out with my black *Monkey Experiment* T-shirt, and my skull-and-crossbones high-tops. Then I do my face with pale foundation, ivory powder, black eye shadow, black eyeliner above and below, black lipstick, and three passes of mascara. I put my copper-colored hair into two ponies just to keep it out of my face.

I don't really make myself up this much when I'm with Mom. She's not a big fan of this look. She says she feels like she's attending my funeral every time she sees me in this makeup. But we hardly see each other anyway.

I grab one of the grocery bags from under the sink, open the front door, and am greeted by something paperish stuck in the screen door.

It's a postcard. On one side is a photo of a Ferris wheel and the words *Greetings From Santa Monica!* I flip it over and see words handwritten in blue ballpoint pen.

Hey, Betty! Meet me at 10. Ignore Alien Orders. Ciao!

I feel something crawling up my spine, but crawling quickly. It's not an iguana or anything like that. It's a feeling.

How does Otis know where I'm staying? Mom would kill me if I hung down with a surfer boy who's practically a surfer man. And it's kinda creepy that he'd want to. But it's kinda incredibly exciting, too, not unlike an iguana crawling quickly up my spine. I don't know why iguana comes to mind, other than that it seems strange and terrifying.

Not that I'm going to meet him at ten, but where does he want to meet? And what does he mean by *ignore alien orders*? Maybe that's some kind of surfer-speak. Like *cowabunga*.

Doesn't matter. Isn't gonna happen. I fold the post-card and put it in my back pocket, so I can throw it away later. Then I come around the hedge and out onto the sunlit sidewalk.

I put the list with Mom's hand-drawn map into my other back pocket, and pull out my phone.

"Siri, find Conscious Consumption."

Siri tells me I need to go several blocks down Fourth Street, then left on Rose. But as I walk, looking down at the route on my screen, before I get to the next block I come upon a section of sidewalk with words that were etched into the cement when it was wet.

IGNORE ALIEN ORDERS.

At the edge of the letters is a pair of bare, suntanned feet, facing my black high-tops. I look up and see the obnoxiously beautiful girl from the ice cream shop, grinning at me.

"Hey, Betty!"

I frown. "My name isn't Betty."

"Oh, I'm *pretty* sure it's Betty."

I scowl. Then it hits me. I'm not sure if it's relief or disappointment. "Did *you* leave that postcard in the screen door?"

"Well, I'm the one standing at Ignore Alien Orders at ten o'clock. Actually you're a little bit late."

She's still smiling. She's the kind of pretty that makes you feel like she's making fun of you, just by looking at you and smiling. I've seen girls like her before, at every school I've been to. But never quite so much as this girl.

"I was just going to the grocery store," I say.

"You didn't come out to meet me?"

"No. I didn't even know these words were here in the sidewalk."

She frowns. "I was sure you'd have seen the words. You seem like the shoe-gazer type."

"I've only been here for one day."

21

"Oh. That explains why I didn't meet you earlier."

I look down at the words. "What does it mean?"

"It means ignore alien orders! Don't listen to what the little green men say. Bossy little devils."

"Did you write it?"

She shakes her head. "It's been here since forever. According to the Big Kahuna. He lives right over there." She points to a bungalow across the street. It's aqua blue with a surfboard leaning against the wall on the front porch.

"Well, excuse me," I say. "I have to get groceries." I begin walking.

"I have to get groceries too!" She follows alongside. "But we should ride our skateboards."

I stop, and turn to her. "Why are you doing this?"

Her smile disappears, and she looks maybe a little hurt. Like maybe there's more to her than just being impossibly happy all the time.

"I thought we could be summer friends," she says. "That's how it's supposed to work with visitors. You come to Ocean Park and get to see the sights, and I get to see *you*."

I feel something strange, light. Like my stomach is smiling. But I furrow my brow. "I don't have a skateboard."

She smiles. "Then we'll walk."

I frown. "Why are you smiling?"

"Because we're going to the grocery store! And because you look so cool made up like a punk-rock corpse doll."

I'm almost certain she's making fun of me, so I don't say thank you. But maybe I smile a very little bit, just in case she meant it.

I start again down the sidewalk, and she walks beside me.

It's strange having her next to me. Except for Fern I haven't walked beside someone my age in forever. And Mom put an end to *that*. So I focus on the screen in my hand, looking at the line between here and there, looking up every few seconds at what we pass.

"You don't need the map app," the girl says. "This neighborhood is home for me. I know where everything is."

I look her up and down, like I've just noticed she's wearing a bikini bottom and a strange swimsuit top that has short sleeves. And nothing else.

"Are they gonna let you in the store like that?"

She makes a screwy face, like my question is absurd. "Of course," she says. "This is *Dog*town."

I have no idea what this means, as I studied the

map carefully before we came, looking for potential hazards, and never saw *Dogtown* anywhere. And I'm pretty sure it's not a good idea for me to be accompanying a girl who doesn't even have a pocket to hold a key or a hundred-dollar bill.

In spite of this, we continue down Fourth Street, in and out of the shade of overhead trees.

"That's where I live," she says, pointing to a blue house with meticulous landscaping. "In that two-story thing that used to be the garage in back."

We pass a school. It seems strange that there are schools here, that this place holds real lives and not just vacation lives.

The sidewalk is narrow and covered in places by mushy berries and strange nutty things that have fallen from the trees above. I'm glad that I'm the one wearing shoes and *she's* the one who's barefoot.

Birds chirp and sing, but no dogs bark. The houses are old and pretty, and very near the sidewalk. The yards are small.

"So, where do you come from?" she asks.

I preferred the sound of her bare feet on the sidewalk. "Just . . . back in the Midwest." It's probably not smart to tell barefoot, strangely cheerful girls your home address.

"What it's like there?" she asks.

I sigh, at least inwardly. Small talk kills me. I'm not very big on *big* talk, either.

"Gross in summer. Cold in winter. Jack-o'-lanterns in fall. Bees in spring."

"That's like a poem," she says.

I shiver. I think I might possibly have metrophobia. That's the fear of poems.

"Left here on Rose," she says. We turn down the street, which has less shade, and small businesses like a yoga studio and a Mexican restaurant. "Anyway," she continues, "it's pretty nice here all the time. It rains some in winter. There's May Gray and June Gloom. It's warmest in September and October when the Santa Ana winds come from the desert, like summer is draining into the ocean."

I shiver again, 'cause that sounded even *more* like a poem.

"July might be the perfect month. The days are long and the sun is warm, so you can always dry off after surfing or boogie boarding. The temperatures stay in the sixties and seventies all month long."

Next she'll probably give me a surf report.

"You don't have many glassy days in July, but the waves can be pretty consistently good. There won't be much more than the occasional nug south of Santa Barbara for the next few days. If you want epic waves, you gotta get up early for dawn patrol."

She stops and looks me up and down. "You surf?"

"You're kidding, right?"

"No waves on the Great Lakes?"

"Not for me."

"Well. Then I'll teach you."

Now *I* smile, because that's definitely not going to happen.

"What are the boys like in the Midwest?"

I shrug. "They're okay. Probably not as cute as the surfer boys here."

"The surfer boys *are* nice to look at," she says. "And to talk shredding with." She quickly bends to pick up a big, shiny leaf, which she hands to me. "But I kinda have a weakness for the nerdy boys who hang out at the library."

I hold the stem of the leaf, twirling it as we walk.

We come upon a section of sidewalk covered in broken green glass.

"Litterbugs!" she exclaims. "Usually the sidewalks are all tidy except for the fruit that keeps falling. Which explains my bare feet."

Cars roll by on Rose. The girl looks around.

"I've got an idea!" she says. "I'll hitch a ride on your kicks!"

Again I have no idea what she's saying. But she steps her right foot onto my left shoe, and her left foot onto my right. Then she puts her arms around me.

"Now hold on to me and walk over the glass." Her beautiful face is inches from mine. Her expression suggests she's about to have the time of her life. "Just walk like Frankenstein so my feet don't come off your shoes."

I can't believe this is about to happen, but I need it to happen fast, because my feet are starting to hurt. I put my arms around her and lift my right foot high like I'm climbing stairs, then move it forward and set it down. Then the same with the left, again and again, until the crunching of glass under my shoes has ceased.

"We did it, Betty!" She steps off my shoes and pushes her Goldilocks hair behind her ears. "Did you tell me your actual name yet? 'Cause I'm gonna be saying it at least some of the time."

She's so *goofy*. I can't help but smile.

"Juillet."

"Joooey Ay?"

"It's like Juliet but the *l*s are silent, and the *e–t* is pronounced like *a–y*. It's French for 'July.'"

Her jaw drops. "No way!" She extends her hand to me. "Summer. That's Ocean Park for *me*."

I give her my hand, which looks pale in hers. "Nice to meet you, Summer."

Another block and we're at Conscious Consumption, a giant grocery store that makes you feel like the more you spend, the more you'll save the planet. Summer starts skipping when we enter, and I have to trot alongside her. She wants to go up and down every aisle looking for samples, and we do, feasting on slices of local black plums and little cubes of local Muenster cheese, and locally roasted cold-brew coffee in tiny paper cups, which the woman who pours thinks is funny we want to try. Then we make the rounds again wearing hats made of hemp that the store sells, pretending to be a new pair of girls who haven't already hit the samples, so we can feast all over again.

We spend almost an hour in the store, smelling food and eating samples and observing the customers. I watch for movie stars. But practically everyone here looks like a movie star.

I feel exhausted by the time we get back to Fourth Street, even though it's barely noon. I'm sore from the walk to and from, and the short distance carrying her weight on my feet, and then cavorting up and down the aisles. But mainly I'm exhausted because my social muscles are weak from not being used, from talking and answering questions, and the odd realization that this girl wants to be spending time with me.

Finally we arrive at the rental cottage.

"So, what's next?" Summer asks. "Wanna hit the waves?"

I pull the key from the coin pocket of my jeans. "Actually, my mom will be here any second. I'm supposed to be doing something with her." I don't know why I'm lying, other than maybe being worn out by Summer's happiness.

"That's so sweet! I hardly ever get to see my mom. She does makeup on movie sets. My dad is a cinematographer for a show on cable, so they're both illusionists. Anyway, she has to take pretty much all the work she can get right now. So we rarely get to spend time together."

I know how *that* feels, but I don't tell her I know how that feels. Mom doesn't need the money so much, but she seems to work as often as she can, ever since Dad left, just so she can stay away from home. I hang out at the mall as much as I can for the same reason. Even though we moved to a new condo to escape the sadness of the house we all lived in together, the furniture is the same, and it feels like we brought the sadness with us.

I put on a smile. "Well, thanks for the tour."

"Ignore Alien Orders at ten o'clock tomorrow?" Her eyebrows arch. She looks so hopeful.

"Okay."

Summer moves in quickly for a hug that's all her. It's not that I don't want to return the hug, but she backs away before I can will myself to raise my arms. "Really you should ignore alien orders at all times, but I'll see you there at ten. Wear your swimsuit!"

I smile, because I don't want to tell her at this moment that there's no way I'm going in the water, and there's no way I'm putting on that mermaid swimsuit again. "See you tomorrow."

Then I go through the screen door and the wooden door to the breezy front room and realize I was so distracted by Summer, I've forgotten to get any groceries whatsoever.

I stand and stare across the living area. The breeze moves through the white curtains, the Beach Boys play from some unseen speaker.

I turn and walk into the kitchen. From the wastebasket beneath the sink I fetch the crumpled list of

Mom's goals for me. I smooth it on the counter, find a pen in a drawer, and add two items to the list.

MAKE A NEW FRIEND
LEARN TO SURF?

I look at what I've written, then crumple it up and throw it back into the wastebasket. Then I take it back out, smooth it once again, and bring it to my room, where I put it in the desk drawer, where it will remain—for my eyes only.

All afternoon I think of the morning with the strange girl, while trying to distract myself with the Cartoon Network. Mom doesn't believe in TV, which is pointless to argue with her about, so we don't have it back home in Lakeshore. But instead of getting lost in the programs here in Ocean Park, I'm thinking of Summer and worrying what she might have planned for tomorrow. I'm worried, but also excited.

Mom brings pad thai home for dinner. I can smell the spicy food as soon as she comes through the door, and it makes me realize how hungry I am.

"How was your day?" She puts the paper takeout bags on the big table.

"It was great." I take the lid off one of the containers, then run to the kitchen for a pair of forks.

"What do you think of the town?" Mom sits, and shakes her head when I offer her a fork. She holds up a pair of chopsticks.

"You can use chopsticks?"

She nods. I didn't know she could use chopsticks.

"Anyway, this neighborhood is really nice. It's pretty, and cheerful, and fun. Like it was made for adventure." I'm talking about Ocean Park, but it feels like I'm talking about Summer. Because *she's* pretty, cheerful, and fun, like *she* was made for adventure.

"It sounds like you had a good day! And it looks like it's giving you a healthy appetite."

I smile through my giant bite of pad thai.

Later we sit on the front porch in the evening air while Mom types medical notes on her laptop.

"Today at the ER there was a guy who accidentally attached his hand to his thigh with a giant screw. It's amazing how many people use power tools on their laps. I guess it could have been worse."

"*Mom.* Please."

"Right, right. Sorry, Juillet. No more horror stories."

Even though she's working, it feels good to be with

her, sharing the same space and the same moment. When she's done on her laptop I tell her more details about my day—the pretty little houses and the pretty little yards, and the mushy berries and nutty things on the sidewalks, and how I passed a school and found myself thinking it's strange that people go to school in such a place, that they do the things that we do when we're home in Lakeshore. But I don't tell her about the girl who left the postcard in the screen door, who ambushed me on the sidewalk, who seemed so happy to tag along with me.

Then I spot a plant growing beside the porch—a fern—which reminds me of the friend I had to leave behind.

"Tell me again why you hate Fern."

Crickets chirp in the bushes beside the porch as Mom thinks of her response. "I don't hate Fern," she says. "It's just that your world has gotten smaller and smaller since you started hanging around her."

"My world is smaller because after Dad left you moved us to a place where I don't know anyone."

She doesn't have an answer for this, so she lets the crickets speak for her.

"I don't know what to do," she says finally. "I'm afraid you're a butterfly who's gone back into her cocoon."

Something in her voice makes me sad, and I feel terrible for making her feel sad. She folds her laptop and goes inside.

I sit in the dark with the crickets and think of how happy Mom would be to hear about Summer, how different she is from Fern, how she's apparently bent on pursuing excitement and adventure. If tomorrow is as good as today was, I might just end up telling Mom about her.

3

THE NEXT MORNING at ten, I'm standing in my swimsuit on the square of sidewalk that says *Ignore Alien Orders*. I put on my mermaid swimsuit without thinking about it, and only realized I had it on when I looked in the mirror. I've been here on the sidewalk for ten minutes, wondering what *ignore alien orders* really means. It's hard to be ten minutes early to someplace ten steps from the door—or maybe twenty steps—but here I am, and here I've been.

Then I see Summer, half a block ahead, turning onto the sidewalk and running my way, grinning.

"Ignore alien orders!" she shouts.

I watch her for a moment, then look across the street to the house she said was the home of someone called the Big Kahuna. I'm not really interested in the

Big Kahuna or his bungalow, or why nobody has stolen the surfboard leaning against the front porch, but it seems weird to be watching Summer all the way up the block, so I don't. Finally she arrives.

"Hey, Betty!" she says, lifting her sunglasses from her eyes to the top of her head. "Are you ready to hit the beach?"

"Do I look ready?" It sounds sort of sarcastic, but I'm genuinely wondering if I look appropriately dressed and otherwise prepared for this horrifying excursion.

"Well, the black high-tops are cute, but we should probably get you some flip-flops if you don't have any."

"Okay."

"And you know I love the punk-rock corpse-doll look, but your makeup is gonna wash off in the surf."

"The surf?"

She doesn't seem to hear me, or notice my worried tone.

"I brought some things for you!" She reaches into a canvas bag. "Stand right where you're standing and don't move!"

First she hands me a sunblock stick.

"Wipe this all over your face. Especially your nose!"

While I'm doing this she moves around me, spraying me with a bottle of Total Eclipse SPF 144 sunscreen until I'm shiny with it.

She takes a gauzy wrap out of the bag and drapes it over my shoulders, and finally a floppy straw hat and dark sunglasses, which she attaches to my head and face. Then she steps back and looks at me. "What's the matter?" she asks.

My shoulders sag. "It's like you're made for the beach, but I look like I've never seen the sun. Like I've been living underground."

She doubles over laughing, but stands up quickly with her hand over her mouth.

"You're so funny!" She picks up her bag. "Anyway, I always use sunscreen. Ready?"

I don't answer, but as she steps toward Ocean Park Boulevard, I follow.

When we get to the corner, we can see all the way down the boulevard past the houses and shops, between the hotels, to the sea.

"It's glassy today," she says.

"Oh." I'm clueless as to what she means by glassy. She seems to have her own vocabulary.

"I wish we were surfing." She stops and turns to me. "What day are you staying until?"

"We leave on July thirty-first. That's my birthday."

"Really?"

"Yeah. I was supposed to be born a week later and be named Augustina. But I came early and they named me Juillet."

"No way! I was named for being born on the summer solstice."

"Really?"

"Yep! I turned thirteen just a couple weeks ago." She smiles, then turns again toward our destination. "Anyway, you staying until the end of the month gives us plenty of time for you to learn to surf."

I don't say anything. I don't want to ruin the beginning of a friendship with a refusal I can make later.

Then I remember that learning to surf is one of the things I wrote on the list of goals.

The sidewalk descends, and my feet slow as we approach the next street. I come to a stop. "Is there another way we can go?"

Summer looks at me, then at the path ahead. "Why?"

I push my sunglasses up my nose. I'm glad they're hiding my eyes.

"There's a mystical adviser at the mall that me and my friend Fern like to go to. She gives us a discounted rate on palm readings and debris divinations."

"Debris divinations?"

"That's where you show her what's at the bottom of your pocket or backpack and she tells you your future.

And she said that she saw my morbid essence shrouded in the number between two and four."

Summer looks confused. "I'm sorry, *who* said this?"

"Mistress Scarfia, Portender of the Obscure. She has a kiosk in front of Softee's Soft Pretzels at Lakeshore Mall." I kick at a pebble. It skips down the sidewalk, down the hill. "She said the number between two and four would be my ruin. I *know* it sounds silly. I don't really believe it, but ever since she said it I've been afraid of that number."

"The number three?"

I nod and look up at the number on the street sign. Even though Mistress Scarfia may just be a phony in purple scarves and beaded necklaces, Mom and Dad and I were a family of between two and four, and now we are two.

"How did you get through to Main Street before?"

I shrug. "My mom is good at distracting me. She's used to me."

Summer reaches up to put her hands on my shoulders. "Well, I wanna get used to you too." She looks around again. I know she's picturing the map in her mind, trying to imagine a way around this street with this number. I've seen Mom do it.

Then she turns back to me, smiling. "I could duct-tape you to my skateboard and roll you down the hill?"

I don't smile, even though it's kinda funny, because it's more embarrassing than funny.

"How about," she begins, "you close your eyes? Then I'll hold your hand and lead you across."

I've come this far. I close my eyes and extend my arm. Her warm hand closes on mine. It's smaller than Dad's, but at least it's here. Dad's big hands are in Switzerland with his ridiculous girlfriend, Genevieve, probably feeding her strawberries dipped in chocolate from a silver platter.

"Baby steps," she says. "A slight downward slope, crossing this street that isn't Third Street."

I smile. "Okay." I hear a car pass slowly by.

"Oh, Betty!" She gets all dramatic, like we're in a movie. "If only you could see the hummingbirds feeding off the blossoms on the stalks above!"

I laugh.

"Really, though," she adds, "there's a ton of them. Ocean Park is like pollinator heaven. Like a hummingbird buffet."

I feel the breeze come up the hill, against my face, lifting the brim of my hat. It *smells* like pollinator heaven, with blossoms whose fragrances are new to my nose.

"Almost there," she says. "Now a slight incline onto

the sidewalk. Shall we go past the dreaded sign?"

"Please."

"Okay. This way a little. Now here comes the miracle. Open your eyes!"

I do.

She's standing before me, smiling brightly. "We did it!"

"We did it." One corner of my mouth turns up. "Thank you."

I feel like a weight has been lifted from me. More because I've told her about one of my fears than the fact that we've gone past the number on the sign. Fear of revealing my fears has been standing between us in my mind ever since the first time at Ignore Alien Orders. Fern is the only other person I talk about them with. But Fern keeps me away from the things I'm afraid of instead of walking me through them.

As for Summer, it's like she's completely forgotten it as we continue down the hill. She's pointing out the things we see.

"That's the little local library branch up there on the right. It's *so* cute. We can go there and you can check out books with my card." She turns to me. "You like to read, right?"

"Yeah."

"I *knew* it. Down on Main Street to the right there's a good breakfast place. Waffles to die for. Do you like waffles?"

"Of course."

She keeps talking, keeps giving me the tour of everything we pass, until we've made it through the little park before the beach, where bikes and skaters roll past on an endless, winding sidewalk, and on to the edge of the sand.

"Here we are! Take off your high-tops."

I'm not really excited about taking my shoes off. When I look at my feet I feel like they belong on somebody else. Somebody *dead*. But Summer makes no remark of them as she pulls the sunscreen from her bag and douses them with spray.

"Let's go!"

The sand is warm but not hot. As we walk, getting closer to the water's edge, the sound of the surf gets louder and louder.

Seagulls cry. The wind tells us to go back, but we don't.

"Also," I say, as Summer drops the canvas bag where the dry sand becomes damp, "I'm afraid of the ocean. I'm afraid of the waves, and the undertow, and rip currents. And tsunamis. Which I realize are not likely."

"Is this also because of Miss Snarfle?"

"Mistress Scarfia. *No.* I'm just afraid of all those things because they can kill you. Even if it isn't likely."

She beams. "It's so brave of you to come here!"

"Unless of course there's an earthquake. In which case tsunamis are a real possibility."

She steps to me and drapes her arms over my shoulders. Again my arms stay stiff at my sides.

"We don't have to do it," she says. "But if you'd like to try it, we could just get our ankles wet. I'll stay by your side."

I think of the list of goals in the drawer at the cottage. *Get outside your comfort zone. Learn to surf.*

"I want to do this." I raise my left hand like a dog ready to shake. She takes it.

I walk beside her, taking little steps. I'm wondering whether she's done this before today, walked beside someone so filled with fear.

"I'm also afraid of sharks," I add.

The sand turns from damp to wet. It feels strange under my feet, different from the shore of the lake back home. Like it's alive.

We keep walking, slowly.

Then the remnants of a small wave roll in. I stop, and hold my breath. My jaw clenches, I squeeze her hand. She squeezes back.

The wave keeps coming. My right foot picks up,

takes a half step back. But I hold my ground, and it comes, the ocean, and it washes over my left foot, then my right, just enough to cover them.

The wave retreats, and the sand beneath my feet crumbles away. Air bubbles appear on the beach where the water has withdrawn. Another wave comes to die at our feet, this one a little bigger, but I stand firm, watching it.

Again and again they come, in rhythm, and I look out to the swimmers and splashers, and watch the waves forming, being born, and coming to us. I watch one march all the way from where the boogie boarders wait for their rides, watch it fight against waves that are on their way back out to sea to be reborn, and watch it all the way up to my toes, my shins, and I laugh.

I look to Summer, and she's watching me. She's *been* watching me—smiling. She squeezes my hand.

"Welcome to Ocean Park," she says. "Welcome to my world."

I'm asleep on the couch when Mom comes home. The opening door wakes me.

"This is a bit early for you to be asleep," she says. "Did you have a big day?"

"Yes." I bite a fingernail. "I've met a new friend."

"Really? That's great!"

"Yeah. Her name is Summer."

"Appropriately enough."

"She lives down the block. She was behind us in line at Pinkie Promise on our first day here."

Mom sets a brown takeout bag on the big table. "What did you guys do?"

"Just ran around. Looked in stores."

I think the whole reason I've told her about Summer is that I feel like I need to reveal *some*thing, but I don't want to tell her about stepping into the ocean, or the street I knowingly crossed to get there. I don't want her to have any more reason to dismiss my fears, to act like they aren't real, because I'm not sure getting my feet wet and crossing that street are experiments I can duplicate. I don't know if I ever want to step into the ocean again, with Mom or Summer or anyone. Mom has been saying that this new me—the girl with the dark makeup, filled with fears—is just a costume I've been putting on every day. I don't want her to think that she's right.

"Well, I'm glad." Mom takes a humongous burrito wrapped in foil from the takeout bag, then cuts it in half. "Are you hungry?"

"Starving."

She asks me questions as we share the gigantic

burrito, and she tells me about her day. I try to listen, and to answer her questions, but I'm momentarily distracted by wondering what Fern would say about what I did today. She might say Summer was trying to get me killed, that I should find some safe mall to hang around instead. And maybe she'd be right to say it, but right now I'm too tired and hungry from a day of adventure to listen to those thoughts.

4

INDEPENDENCE DAY. SUMMER said she would be busy today but didn't say why. Since I don't have any other plans or any kind of idea how to entertain myself in this town without her, I hang around the house and the little table outside behind the tall hedge, listening for her skateboard, watching for a flash of her golden hair, even though she said she wouldn't be around. She never appears.

Finally I decide to take a walk.

I'm dressed in jeans and my black *Graveside Lobotomy* T-shirt. Graveside Lobotomy is one of my favorite bands. Their song "Let's Switch Brains" kills me. I've gone light on the Goth makeup, maybe just because the black gets hot and kinda melty in the sun here. That doesn't really happen when you're hanging out in the mall like I do back home, but it does here in Ocean Park on the bright sidewalks and at the beach.

I walk down the hill, staying under the shade of trees on Ocean Park Boulevard as much as I can. I stop at the next block down and consider the street sign with the number that should not be spoken.

It doesn't jump at me, the street itself doesn't crack open and swallow me up. Above, a swarm of humming-birds dart among the blossoms in a strange plant that has towering stalks with flowers two stories high, like something drawn by Dr. Seuss. It's exactly the scene Summer described yesterday when I went through it with my eyes closed, coming and going.

Instead of crossing the street, I turn around and go back up the hill. I only wanted to see the hum-mingbirds anyway. I play the idea in my mind until I practically believe it. But I remember the list in the drawer in the cottage, and I turn around from the top of the hill.

"I'm not afraid of you!" I shout down the hill to the sign. "Number three. Say it three times. Three three three."

A guy on a bike rides by and smiles. I feel my embar-rassment glowing in my face. I turn down Fourth Street and think of Mistress Scarfia. She's really just a sad old woman with warts on her nose who eats pretzels from Softee's every day for lunch.

There's not as much to do on Fourth Street as there is at the bottom of the hill on Main Street and beyond. But I stop at the little market and get an Orange Sunshine soda—not my usual flavor—then take it to the park on the top of the hill, which has a big expanse of grass and tall, shady trees, and a view of the ocean in the distance. If there were a tsunami, this park would be a good place to be, high above sea level. From here I could see it all, see the destruction unfold from a safe distance. I think of this and wonder what you do after you witness the destruction of everything but aren't a part of it.

Fern and I spend a lot of time talking about the end of the world, and what it will be like. At the mall we talk about what would happen to the stores and everything in them, depending on whether the end comes from asteroids or zombies or plague, and which stores we'd loot, since everyone would be freaking out and not paying for anything.

Mom thinks it isn't normal to spend so much time thinking about the end of the world, and she thinks Fern brings it out in me. She thinks I've become obsessed with the apocalypse because I don't want to think about the fact that my dad left us and ruined our lives, but his leaving proves that things do fall apart.

It's just a matter of what's gonna fall apart next. Or maybe everything is gonna fall apart at once. And even though nothing particularly bad has happened to Fern, she still understands that it's only a matter of time.

All of that seems a world away as I sit on the cool green and examine tiny white flowers that grow scattered above the grass. Then I notice a homeless man lying on the ground. He props himself up on his elbows, not even a hundred feet from me. He's shoeless, and even from this distance I can see that the soles of his feet are black with street tar.

He catches me staring at him and grins. More like a half grin, because he's missing half his teeth. I quickly look away. Then I feel bad about looking away, like he's got bubonic plague and I can catch it from staring at him or whatever. Or that what he is can rub off on me. I look back so I can smile at him, like *Isn't this a lovely day sir*, but he's lain back down. A couple of moms and a dad are having a playgroup with toddlers nearby, but they don't seem bothered by the homeless man at all. They don't seem to notice him a bit.

I watch as the dad in the playgroup lifts his toddler daughter to the sky. She laughs down at him. Then he turns her around and puts her on his shoulders. I feel a twinge of pain in my heart, thinking of *my* dad and everything he used to do with me. Rides on his shoulders. Lifting me into trees to inspect the newly budding leaves. Teaching me to ice-skate, reading stories to me at bedtime. Sitting in the front row at my piano recitals, beaming. Holding my hand whenever I was afraid. Holding my hand so I was never afraid.

Dad is the reason I play the piano. It was his ambition as a kid, but then he chose medical school over music, because his parents wanted him to be practical. He still plays, and he plays really well, but he's laid his ambition at my feet. Now that he's gone, every time I see a piano, or hear the notes coming from it, my heart hurts.

I look away from the playgroup. The breeze moves through my hair. My phone buzzes, and I take it from my back pocket to check it.

It's a text from Fern.

Why does your mom hate me? I miss you. The mall isn't the same without you.

She used to text me constantly. But the longer it's been since Mom forbade me communicating with Fern, the less often she does. It's like I'm seeing her give up on me in slow motion. Her texts and her lonely words make me feel guilty, because the reason we can't see each other is totally my fault. So I lie on the grass and try to think of something else.

Instead I think of the times we spent together.

Once we were at the mall, sitting in the food court, eating soft pretzels and watching boys.

"You know, the music they play here has messages in it to make you buy more stuff." She tore a bit off a soft pretzel and dipped it in the spicy mustard.

"Really?"

"Yeah. The words are backward but your brain can figure it out without you even knowing."

I tried to imagine what *buy more stuff* would sound like backward. *Futs rom yub?*

"It's all science." She took a sip of lemonade. "Come on! It's too noisy in the food court. But if we sit directly under a speaker in a quiet part of the mall I bet we'll be able to hear it."

She pulled me away from the table. I grabbed my lemonade and followed her. We passed the Athlete's Foot, the shoe store where the cute guy at the register wears the referee uniform, and the music store where the grim man in the suit plays the organ at the store entrance. I wondered if maybe the grim man playing the organ was in on the hidden-message thing, too.

Finally Fern stopped at a couch surrounded by fake plants with a speaker overhead.

"Now we sit with our eyes closed and listen."

At the park in Santa Monica, I close my eyes and listen, remembering the day at the mall with Fern. At the mall there were no birds singing. There wasn't the sound of the breeze moving through the trees. Just fake light and fake air, and music she said would make us want to buy things.

After fifteen minutes, Fern said she had an urge to buy a family-size set of luggage, but I didn't feel anything. I didn't feel anything at all. So Fern insisted we stay and listen another fifteen minutes. By then I was late for piano practice, and Mom was not happy.

Being late for piano practice wasn't why I was banned from seeing or speaking to Fern. Mom put an end to my friendship with Fern because of a lie I told. Mom doesn't even know it was a lie, and if I had told the truth—or if I told the truth now—I could still be friends with Fern. But I don't want to tell the truth, or even think about it, even from this distance, in a beautiful park high above the apocalypse.

I stand and take my empty soda can to a recycling bin, then make my way back to the cottage. It's still empty, still nobody home, and it occurs to me how much I'm missing Summer.

I go back to the screen door to make sure there isn't a note or postcard that I've missed. There isn't.

I walk into my bedroom and open the desk drawer. The list is staring back up at me, beside a little pencil. I take them both and flatten the list on the desktop. I stare out the open window. A hummingbird stops in front of me, hanging in midair. He nods, then moves on.

Putting the pencil tip to the list, I make an addition.

FIX FERN THING

I watch a marathon of cartoons, eight episodes of the same show. Every time I hear a skateboard pass, I run to the window. They don't really sound like *her* skateboard, but I do it anyway. It's never Summer. I would text her just to say *what's up*, but she told me she doesn't have a service plan anymore. Summer didn't say why she doesn't have a service plan. But she just has an ancient phone with a cracked screen, and all she does is take pictures with it. I've got a service plan but nobody to text.

Mom said she'd pick me up at six thirty and take me to dinner at a Vietnamese place on Main Street. I save my appetite for it, holding off on snacks after lunch. Now it's 6:47 and I'm starving.

At 7:02 I finally hear the screen door open, and I reach for my shoes. But then there's a knock on the door.

I don't like answering doors, especially in a city like Los Angeles. Technically Santa Monica, but surrounded by the much more menacing LA. And now with the sun lower, the shadows lengthening. So I sit completely still on the couch. I even hold my breath.

"Betty!"

I almost fall off the couch in surprise, then look up to see Summer's smiling face at the little window by the door that lets in the breeze. Her face is practically in the living room.

"Don't do that!" I say, getting to my feet.

"Did you order a pizza? 'Cause I have one!"

I unlock the door and open it. She comes through with a giant pizza box. It's so big she practically has to turn it on its side to get in the door. She's wearing a long-sleeve hoodie and jeans.

"I'm going out to dinner with my mom," I say. Then my stomach growls. "But maybe I could have just one slice."

"This place is so cute!" Summer puts the pizza on the table and opens the top of the box. "Spinach and garlic! Six slices for me and six for my new bestie." She pulls up a chair.

I'm sure she doesn't mean it about me being her new best friend. But the pizza smells incredible. I'm drooling like a dog. I fetch plates and napkins from the cupboard. I also pour two glasses of water, then join her at the table.

"Where did this come from?" I take my first bite. It's heavenly.

Summer closes the lid and looks at the top of the box. It's got a picture of an Italian-looking guy with a mustache and a chef's hat, smiling and giving a thumbs-up. And the name of the pizzeria. "Gino's. I *love* Gino's!"

"You couldn't remember where you got it?"

"It was a gift from a delivery guy," she says through a mouthful of pizza. "*Gratis*, as they say in old Italy. Or is that Spanish? Anyway, he had one of those delivery bicycles with a big basket on the front. But he said he'd just decided to quit and did I want a pizza?"

I set my slice down. "So you just accepted a pizza from a stranger without question?"

She swallows the last of her bite, then licks tomato sauce from her lips. "Of course not! I asked if it was vegetarian first. And anyway, delivery people are pretty much always strangers. Right? Unless you have friends who deliver pizza. Which would be very cool."

"What if it's poisoned?"

"It's probably not. If it is, then at least it's also delicious." She takes another bite.

"But at least you *know* Gino's Pizza. I mean, you've

eaten there before." I study her expression. "Right?"

"Actually, I've never heard of them."

"You said you loved them!"

"I do! Or at least I do *now!*" She takes another bite and talks through it. "And it's *so* good, huh? But what if the owners were mean to the delivery guy? Maybe that's why he was quitting."

My head spins with worries.

Summer shakes her head. "Nah, he said he was quitting because he wanted to watch the fireworks on the beach. Which brings me to why I'm here."

"Fireworks?"

She lays another slice in front of me. "Yeah. Eat up!"

"Fireworks begin with the word *fire.* They also include explosions. And showers of sparks, which are technically small fires."

"Sounds like you've figured out the science behind why they're so beautiful." She bares her teeth in a grin and tears off a huge bite, then again speaks with her mouth full. "Hurry! I gotta get made up for the celebration." She holds up a little makeup bag and shakes it.

I look at the pizza before me. "My mom will be here any minute."

"We won't be all night. And this only happens once every year!"

It's killing me watching her eat, I'm so famished. Maybe I'd rather die from eating possibly poisoned pizza given by an outlaw former pizza-delivery guy than from hunger. I pick up my slice.

Summer takes a gulp of water. "What did you say your mom does?"

I look at the clock on the wall. "She's an emergency-room doctor. She's teaching at a hospital in Los Angeles for a month. It's part of the same system as the hospital back home."

Summer spreads her hands palms down on the table and leans toward me. "Can we just leave her a couple slices and go see the fireworks?"

I look away, toward the door. "She'll be here any minute."

I keep saying that, and I keep eating the pizza. So does Summer, and finally it's 7:29 and there are only two more slices for Mom.

"She probably got held up at the hospital," I say. "You can't just walk away when someone's bleeding to death. And she can't really take out her phone to text me when she's putting someone back together." I hear a car, but it drives by. My heart rises and sinks, that quickly. "I shouldn't bail on her. We made plans."

"I'd love it if you'd watch the fireworks with me. We'll be at a very safe distance. They're way down at the Marina and we'll be on the beach. But we'll keep our feet dry. I'm not even wearing a bathing suit."

The stupid list in the drawer calls out to me. *Go outside your comfort zone.*

Finally I give up on Mom arriving, or I agree with Summer, so I text Mom that I'm leaving, and Summer and I walk down to the beach to watch explosions and showers of fire. Summer has poster-paint red lipstick, bright blue eye shadow, and tiny white sticker stars in her hair and on her face. Ordinarily I would say that kind of thing is ridiculous, but she looks adorable. I've got my usual Goth face on, and I'm kinda jealous of hers. Almost.

We wait to cross Main Street at the light. Two guys our age roll up on skateboards. They look us up and down as they wait beside us.

"Hey, Summer," the smirkier-looking of the two says in an unfriendly tone. "What's up?"

"Nada." Obviously they know each other, but Summer is acting like she doesn't want to talk to them.

"You're looking all God-bless-America," the talker says. "And where'd you find your friend? The graveyard?" The other boy laughs a mean, filthy laugh.

The light is still red. Beneath the makeup my face burns, as I feel their eyes on me, up and down.

"What are you lookin' at?" Summer finally says,

standing straight and taking a step toward them. "My friend is a better surfer than you'll ever be, you goofy-footed posers."

The light turns green, and the skaters roll across the street, shaking their heads.

"Stupid hodads." Summer shakes her head. I make a mental note to google *hodad* as we start across the street.

"Who are they?"

"My nemesis, Wade, and his stupid sidekick who laughs at everything he says."

"Do they go to your school?"

She changes her canvas beach bag from one shoulder to the other. We reach the other side of Main Street and continue down the sidewalk on Ocean Park Boulevard. "School's been tricky."

I glance at Summer as we duck under a low branch hanging over the sidewalk. She looks like she doesn't want to expand on her answer.

"I said that thing about you being a better surfer than them just to get under their skins," she says. "But it's okay if you don't ever learn to surf. You're still way cooler than they are." Then she stops and turns to me. "Also, if you *do* surf and you end up being goofy-footed, that's perfectly fine."

I nod. "Thanks."

I have no idea what it means, but I hope like heck I'm not goofy-footed.

We pass the last couple of blocks and enter the park. Coming down the sidewalk, a noisy procession of people dances as they make their way to the south. Most of them are laughing and singing. We watch as we wait for them to pass. Many are wearing white robes, and some play instruments like a trumpet or tambourine. Some of the guys have shaved heads.

They terrify me.

"I love watching Hare Krishnas," Summer says.

"Why?"

"They look so happy. They *sound* so happy. Blowing horns and beating drums, and dancing. They're probably going down to Venice to have a party." She turns to me. "Venice is kooky. It's the best."

"Aren't you afraid you'll get sucked into it? Like, you'll become one of them and the next time I see you you'll be passing out pamphlets on a curb somewhere?"

Summer laughs, and puts her hand over her mouth. "When you go to the zoo are you afraid you'll become a monkey?" Then she tries to look serious. "I'm sorry— is that one of your fears?"

"No." I try to make my eyebrows frown to counter the smile that appears on my face. "It's not the same. Monkeys don't try to recruit you."

"It's *practically* the same. Come on!"

The Hare Krishnas have passed, and we cross over the sidewalk, through to the sand of the beach. We get close to the water so we have a clear view to the south. We spread the blanket Summer brought onto the sand.

"There used to be bonfires on the beach," she says. "But they banned them because of the smoke." She lies back on the blanket and sighs. "Dude, that pizza ruined me. Wake me up when the fireworks start."

I briefly consider the possibility that she *has* in fact been poisoned by the pizza, that we've *both* been poisoned by it. Then I decide she's just sleepy from so much food. She doesn't actually go to sleep, but just lies there with her eyes closed. Meanwhile I watch people on the beach—playing in the water, settling down in the sand to watch fireworks.

The sun plunges into the Pacific. The lights twinkle brighter on the shoreline, all the way up to Malibu, where the mountains spill into the sea.

Finally I lie beside her.

"I'm *so* glad we met," she says.

Then a red light ascends high into the sky to the

south, and explodes in a shower of sparks that look like a spider with too many legs.

"Me too."

The *boom* reaches us, and Summer props herself up on her elbows. I follow suit. Seconds later the fully darkened sky fills with blossoms of sparks.

"Oooooh," Summer says, smiling. I watch her profile. I watch the show of fireworks, safely reflected in her eyes.

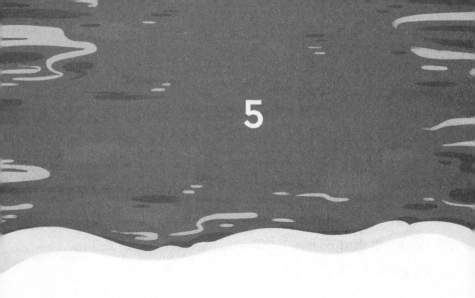

5

I WAKE TO birdsong drifting through the open window. It's early enough that the marine layer is still filtering the sunlight, softening it. Summer says the marine layer is the name for the low clouds that hang around the coast from the morning until they burn off before noon. She says in May and June the clouds sometimes hang around all day, but in July they pretty much always burn off eventually.

I've got a knot in my stomach because I told Summer I'd wade into the water with her today. Like, not just my feet and shins. I'm so nervous I can't even finish my bowl of cereal.

After ignoring alien orders, after we walk down the hill to the beach, I'm standing beside Summer in my mermaid swimsuit at the water's edge.

"I think it's best just to walk in like you own it," she says. "Don't let it even guess you might be afraid of it."

I bite a fingernail. "How far in could a shark possibly come?"

She shrugs. "Not any farther than the snack shack."

I turn and look at it, standing in the distance by the sidewalk.

"I'm kidding!" She pokes me. "We'll be fine. But do you want to hold my hand?"

"It's embarrassing. Like I'm a baby." But I *am* a baby.

"How about we pretend we're holding hands because we're friends?"

"Okay."

"Like we just met a few days ago, but already we love hanging out."

I look at my feet. "Okay."

"Like when we're apart we can't wait to be together again."

I'm not sure if she's serious or joking. Or whether she can read my mind and she's kidding me about it. I smile anyway. "Okay."

Summer holds out her hand. I hold out mine, and she takes it.

"Just goin' in for a little splishy-splashy," she announces to anyone in hearing range. "Gettin' the old gills wet."

This makes me laugh, and takes my mind off the fear. We walk down the slope of the beach. The water invades the space between our toes.

"Probably not walking all the way to China," she says. "Maybe just up to our thighs."

I look down to see how high the water is. It's only halfway to my knees.

Then a girl approaches us from the deeper water. She trudges toward the shore, her hair completely wet.

"Gidget!" Summer shouts. *"Wassup?"*

"Hey, Summer! Just getting a little swimming in." She's actually a grown woman—not very tall, but she looks like a professional athlete. "Sitting out these ankle busters?"

"Yeah, not worth bringing our boards today. This is Juillet, aka Betty. Betty, this is Gidget."

Gidget smiles and offers a fist for me to bump, like the jock boys do back home. I punch at it uncomfortably with my free hand.

Gidget kicks at the water. "Maybe tomorrow'll be better."

"Dude!" Summer gestures toward the ocean laid before us. "It couldn't be any choppier than this."

"You shoulda been here yesterday." Gidget looks down at our joined hands and smiles. "Later." She does this thing with her thumb and pinkie, wagging them back and forth, then walks past us, up the shore.

I look down at my free hand. I make a fist except for my thumb and pinkie.

"That's the shaka," Summer says. "It means 'hang loose.' But you gotta waggle it."

I try.

Summer smiles. "You got it."

I look out to the water. "She could tell I'm afraid."

"Gidget? What makes you think that?"

"She saw my hand holding yours. Then she smiled."

Summer gives me a little frown. "Maybe she's just happy to see me with a friend."

I don't know what to say, so I don't say anything.

We move forward into the water. It climbs past my knees. A wave rolls in and advances up my thighs, but I hardly notice. I hardly notice because I'm thinking that obviously a girl like Summer would have plenty of friends.

I hold my ground as the waves try to push us toward the shore and tug us toward the deep. The water moves up and down our legs while fearless toddlers splash around us, attacking the waves, then retreating. Seagulls fly down the coast, then four pelicans in formation, and a lifeguard helicopter.

The sun glints off the water. The breeze blowing in from the blue-green distance smells like adventure, but I'm not turning away from it. I gaze out in the distance to a yacht cruising beyond the breakwater, then down to the hand holding mine.

6

THE NEXT DAY Summer is busy, so I'm solo until we ignore alien orders at six p.m. and take the Big Blue Bus down Fourth Street to Colorado. The plan is to go to the pier. As we ride the shiny new bus with its cushiony seats, I'm thinking of all the things that could go wrong on this excursion. For starters, the pier is a big thing made of wood sticking way out into the ocean. I went online earlier to preview the terrifying experience that awaits me, and to look at pictures of the rides that are on the pier. They would be scary enough if they were built on solid, dry ground, but they're made worse by the fact that they're on a wooden platform over a roiling ocean that would love to smash it all to bits.

We get off the bus near the train station, and the

sidewalks are thick with people who've ridden to the end of the Expo Line in Santa Monica from various parts of Los Angeles to do exactly the kind of touristy thing that Summer and I are about to do.

I'm wearing a black T-shirt that says *DEATH* in big white letters. In this case it's not the name of one of my favorite bands, or any band that I'm aware of. It's just what ends up happening to all of us eventually. Summer laughed when she saw it, but she said it looked super cute on me. I'm also wearing my favorite ripped jeans and my black high-tops. I went a little bit light on the black makeup.

She, meanwhile, is wearing a light blue hoodie that says *Um okay*. People we pass look from me to Summer, from Summer to me, and smile like we're telling some kind of joke. Like Happy is taking Sad for a walk.

When we get to Second Street she stops suddenly.

"Wait. Can we go back? I wanna show you the promenade. It's the old street we just passed. Cars aren't allowed and it has all these shops and restaurants and performers on it. And movie theaters!"

I give her a look of dread.

"Yes," she confesses. "Yes, it is in fact Third Street, but nobody calls it that, and there's so much happening you won't even think about it. Come on!"

70

She leads me back through throngs of people on the sidewalk. We turn onto the promenade. Like she said, it's filled with people and stores and places to eat. There's a fortune-teller, and a woman singing and playing guitar for hat money, and someone with a monkey on a leash, all on the first block. It's like a mall, but with sea breeze and sky and birds.

My phone buzzes. It's a text from Mom.

WHERE ARE YOU? I GOT AN ALERT THAT YOU CROSSED THE BOUNDARY.

"Ugh. My mom always texts in all caps, so it feels like she's shouting at me. But she might actually be shouting this time."

Summer waits while I text back.

Me and Summer are about a hundred feet north of Colorado on the promenade. Just looking at things. Then we are going to the pier, safely tucked within the boundary. Bye!

"She's tracking me on her phone." I stuff mine into my back pocket.

Summer smiles. "That's sweet."

"It's annoying. She says she wants me to go outside my comfort zone, but I bump into the limits of *her* comfort first."

Summer lets her smile fade. She gestures down the block. "I need to show you something."

I follow Summer down the promenade. She slows as we approach a fountain surrounded by landscaping, with bushes trimmed to the shapes of dinosaurs. Then she points to a sketchy-looking guy holding a camera. He's got a scrawny goatee and dark sunglasses.

"This guy will take our picture for five bucks!"

"Why don't we just do a selfie with our phones for free?"

"These are Polaroids! They develop right away. They're more fun!"

Summer lets go of my hand, peels off a five, and gives it to the creepy guy.

"Over here!" she says. "Let's do it with the fountain behind."

The goatee guy follows us. Summer's steps get smaller as we near the fountain. Then she turns. She looks over her shoulder at the spray, then to the guy with the camera. "This is close enough, right?"

He shrugs.

We stand side by side. I feel Summer's shoulder against mine.

The guy with the camera kneels on one knee before us. "Smile." He says it without cheer.

The flash flashes before the smile reaches my face. I feel Summer's hand close over mine.

"Did you get a good shot?" she calls out.

But he's already pulling the photo from the camera as he approaches. "You'll know in a minute." He hands it to Summer and turns away.

Summer drops the photo in her bag before it develops. "Come on, let's get to the pier so we can watch the sunset!" She leads me off the promenade, down the sidewalk.

We cross a busy street called Ocean, and enter a narrow strip of green park on the bluffs overlooking the beach and the endless sea beyond. We follow it to a bridge that takes us over the Pacific Coast Highway and the sand, and onto the pier.

The bridge and the pier are packed with people. They all walk out onto the pier, mill around on it, and then walk away from it. In between they buy food and souvenirs and ride the rides at Pacific Park—the name of the little amusement park on the pier—and cast their fishing lines into the ocean, and watch performers, and stare out to sea.

"Look at this!" Summer says. She leads me to a guy at a cart with a sign that says *Your Name Painted on a*

Grain of Rice. The guy supposedly paints your name on a grain of white rice and then puts it in a tiny glass vial with a little cork on the opening, and charges you twenty bucks for it. But you would need a stupidly powerful magnifying glass to even see it.

"I wanna get one with *your* name on it!" Summer says.

I smile. "I can get one with *your* name on it."

But then Summer gets distracted by a homeless man standing nearby. Dirty and bearded, he's leaning back against the railing. Hanging from his neck is a sign with big, hand-drawn words.

MY TALE OF WOE WRITTEN ON A GRAIN OF RICE. DONATIONS CHEERFULLY ACCEPTED

Summer pulls me to him.

The homeless man holds a fishing pole with a line dangling from it, to which he's attached a tiny glass vial with a grain of rice inside. Hanging below that is a paper cup that's been torn shorter, with a few dollars sticking out of it.

Summer moves closer and examines the vial. She squints at the grain of rice.

"How do I read it?" she asks.

He shrugs, then speaks in a growl. "Prob'ly a

magnifying glass. Or a microscope."

"Have you *got* a magnifying glass or a microscope?"

He shakes his head.

"If I give you some money, will you *tell* me your tale of woe?" she asks.

The homeless man rolls his eyes, like he'd rather just cash in on his gimmick, which really is pretty good as far as gimmicks go.

"Once I had everything," he begins in his gravelly voice.

"Wait!" Summer says. "What's your name?"

He rolls his eyes again. *"Butch."*

"Okay. Sorry. Please continue, Butch."

"Once I had everything. A philosophy degree, a dog that followed me everywhere, and a sleeping bag. And then . . ."

He pauses, and looks over his shoulder, over the railing of the pier, like he's expecting to see something in the water below. He turns back to us, and stares at the wooden beams of the platform in front of him, his brow furrowed.

"Then what?" Summer asks.

"Then I ran out of room on the grain of rice."

Summer looks at me and grins. But I don't grin back because I feel like somehow it's mean for her to look happy.

"That's a real cliff-hanger," she tells him. "But I really care about the character. And it makes me want to know what happens to Butch next." She puts the twenty-dollar bill she's been holding into the cup on the end of the fishing line, and gives the string a tug. "I think you've got a bite!"

Then she looks over her shoulder at the Ferris wheel, and turns to me, raising her eyebrows, asking without words.

Even though the sight of the Ferris wheel is horribly frightening, even though it goes against everything in my entire body, from my nerve endings to my brain, suddenly I feel like I want to stay at Summer's side, wherever she takes me. I don't know why, but I feel like I'll follow her, even if it means tagging along on the Ferris wheel, in a tiny cup on a rickety wheel high above the frothy ocean. So I smile my consent, and Summer smiles back and leads me there.

The line for the Ferris wheel is long, and it gives me plenty of time for regrets. The thick wooden planks beneath our feet make me feel like we're on a pirate ship. They make me feel like I'm about to walk the plank.

A roller coaster roars overhead every minute or so, and the people on it scream in terror. They wait in line to scream in terror. Screaming in terror is why everyone is here.

Finally it is our turn to enter the metal cup that will take us around and around, from the pier to the sky. We step in, we sit down.

There is no seat belt. Just physics keeping us inside the little cup, and the hope that the wheel doesn't bust loose from its moorings and roll into the sea.

Summer smiles, the wheel lurches and begins moving. Up we go.

I feel the ocean breeze in my face and hair, but I won't look outside the cup we sit in. Instead I'm looking at my folded hands between my knees.

Summer scoots over and sits beside me. Her jeans are against mine. Then she puts one arm across my shoulders, and holds me close.

"Do you want to look? It's really beautiful."

I don't say anything, but I don't want to look. Then I do anyway. Slowly, slowly I raise my head, my eyes, and look to where the sinking sun shines off the surface of the sea. Summer squeezes my shoulder, and my heart leaps. Because it *is* beautiful. *All* of it. It makes my heart ache, and chills run down my spine.

The distant mountains that jut out into the water are backlit and misty. Nearer, just beyond the pier along the beach, I can see the waves being born, and the surfers who want to love the waves, lined up, waiting to claim them.

And, nearest, Summer's smile, and my own smile reflected in her sunglasses. I look happy. Maybe I really am.

The wheel goes around and around, and then, like the sun, we come down, and everything is golden.

7

THE NEXT DAY, early afternoon, the sun is warm.

"Okay," Summer says. "You ready?"

We're standing side by side at the water's edge, both in bikinis. Mine is brand-new, bought on the pier last night.

"Can you remind me again what it is I'm supposed to be ready for?" I watch as a wave advances and reaches my toes.

Summer smiles. "We're gonna walk toward the horizon until either your feet are off the ocean floor or your head is underwater."

I sigh. "And what again is the point of that?"

"Swimming. Ideally you'll choose to have your feet leave the ocean floor and you'll begin swimming. But feel free to dip your head underwater too."

"I already know how to swim."

"Of course!" She grins. "So this will be easy."

But it *won't* be easy, because this body of water is endlessly vast, unfathomably deep, filled with a million creatures I don't want to meet.

"Let's take a walk," she says. She steps forward, then keeps stepping, and rather than be left behind, I follow by her side.

Quickly the water is above our knees. Summer doesn't give me a chance to object.

We're waist-deep. A wave moves against us.

"Cold!" I bark.

"Fresh from the Gulf of Alaska. The cold current is why the air doesn't get hot on the coast all summer."

We keep moving forward. There's a sudden drop, a quick downward slope. A wave comes and I jump up to keep my head dry, but Summer dives beneath it. She comes up looking like it's the best thing she's ever done, like she's in a commercial for this, shimmering as the water runs from her golden hair.

"Getting deep," she says. "Ready for liftoff?"

I don't answer, but the next wave comes and I lean forward. I try to breaststroke into it like at the pool at the country club back home, but it pelts me, mashing my face and hair. I'm swimming, though, and wet from head to toe. Mission accomplished.

"Woo-hoo!" Summer shouts. "Follow me!"

I do follow, for a while, but we're getting too far out. Summer said it doesn't matter how deep the ocean is once you're swimming, but it doesn't feel that way to me right now. Deeper feels deeper.

"I wanna go back!" I shout. I turn and head to shore.

But as hard as I swim, I feel like I'm getting nowhere. The shore seems to be growing more distant instead of nearer.

I keep swimming at the shore but not getting closer to it. I'm getting tired. A lifeguard on the beach waves her arms like she wants me to go to my left, but I want to come in.

I look over my shoulder at Summer. She's way far out now, but she's waving too. She's waving at me to move the same way the lifeguard is, because she doesn't understand, either. I turn back toward the beach. I kick and paddle as hard as I can, but it's like I'm trying to swim upstream against a river's current. My shoulders are tired, my thighs are burning, my feet are cramping. I'm out of breath.

I start to panic. It's like when I was a little girl at the mall and I accidentally started going down an escalator, away from Mom and Dad, and I tried to step back up, but the escalator kept carrying me down, and no matter how fast I tried to run up I couldn't get closer to them. Finally Dad smiled and stepped down the escalator, picked me up, held me. But he's half a world away and not getting any closer, and though my arms dig and my legs kick, my breaths coming in gasps, the shore isn't getting any closer, either.

Suddenly I'm face-to-face with an angel—a lifeguard, a woman, who looks like Summer if Summer were an adult and had brown hair.

"Rest," she says. "I got you. You're safe."

She pushes her flotation device at me. I grab hold of it, and my legs fall toward the ocean floor. I stop kicking and immediately feel myself drifting more quickly out to sea.

"This is a rip current," she says. "No sense in trying to swim against it. It's moving straight out from the beach. What we want to do is move laterally until we're no longer in it." She rolls onto her back and begins a lazy backstroke. "Stay by my side, nice easy kicks. Let the current push you away from shore, and meanwhile we'll kick our way *out* of the current, down the beach toward the pier."

She stays by my side, watching me.

"Beautiful," she says. "You're doing great. Just a little bit farther and we'll be out of the current."

I swim blindly, staying by her side. Then suddenly

I don't feel like I'm being pulled out to sea anymore.

"You're safe." She smiles. "When we wave at you with our rescue buoys, pointing up or down the beach, that most likely means there's a rip current. They can come out of nowhere. You can't fight 'em. You just gotta get out of 'em."

"Okay."

"And trust Summer. If she waves at you to move down the beach, then do as she advises. She's a smart surfer. A smart swimmer."

"Okay."

"Betty!" Summer appears. "Are you okay?" She looks more scared than I was.

"I'm okay," I say. But I start crying.

"I'm so sorry," Summer says. "I should have stayed closer to you."

"You two are pretty shook up," the lifeguard says. "Why don't you come in and take a break? Betty can borrow my buoy until we get to shore."

"Thanks, Heather." Summer still sounds choked up. "You're the best."

"*You're* the best," the lifeguard says. "I'm just doing my job."

We kick to the beach, but now it's easy. Especially for me with the buoy. The sun is warm on my back, the beach and the town bask before us.

But as we pass the waders standing near the shore, they stare at me. I'm the girl who needed to be rescued. So I keep my eyes to myself.

Feet on the sand, I hand the buoy to lifeguard Heather, and thank her. Summer gives her a hug, so I give her a hug too.

Summer and I have to walk down the beach a hundred yards to find our towels spread in the sand. I drop onto mine. Summer sits beside me.

"You're a strong swimmer," Summer says.

"Are you kidding?"

"No. You fought that rip current for ages."

I look down at the sand. "That makes me strong but stupid."

"No. That's totally my bad. This is new to you. I should have stayed by your side. I should have told you about rip currents." She scoops sand over her feet to bury them. She shakes her head.

I scoop sand to bury my own feet like Summer did hers, though I'm not sure why. Then I look out to the sea, which just tried unsuccessfully to claim me. A shiver hits me—either from the cold water, fresh from the Gulf of Alaska—or because there's something exhilarating about being afraid of something that's really real.

A little later we're at a taco shop on Main Street, dry suited and salty haired, sitting on the patio in the afternoon breeze. A woman walking by stops beside our table.

"Mom!" Summer says. *"Wassup?"*

The woman smiles and looks from Summer to me, then back to Summer. "Hello, Summer. Who's your friend?"

I stand and extend my hand. "Hi, I'm Juillet."

She smiles, shakes my hand. It's like looking at Summer in thirty years. But maybe a sadder Summer who doesn't have time to ride waves anymore.

"It's nice to meet you, Juillet."

"Her name is Betty!" Summer interjects.

"*My* name is Anna," she says. "Do you live here in town?"

"She's visiting from Michigan!" Summer says. "Fireflies, snowmen. Did you say snowmen?"

Summer is acting silly, but the sadness underlying her mom's expression grows deeper. "Oh. Well, then I guess we only get to enjoy you for a short while."

"Until the end of July," I say. "Summer's been show-ing me around."

"Betty's gonna learn to surf!" Summer says.

"Good." She looks at her watch. "Summer, did you say you were out of conditioner? I have to pick up some things for Hank at the pharmacy."

Summer frowns. "Of course you do."

Her mom watches her. "Well? Are you out of conditioner?"

Summer looks away. "No. *Yes*. Whatever."

Her mom forces a smile at me. "It was nice meeting you, Juillet. Good luck catching a wave."

I force a smile back. "It was nice meeting you, too. And thank you."

"Bye, Mom. Sorry for being . . . you know."

"It's fine. I have to be on set tonight, so I won't see you." She bends down to kiss Summer, waves to me, then walks away with the same gait as her daughter.

I stare at my guacamole, then pick up a chip. "Is everything okay?"

Summer raises her veggie taco. "Everything is perfect." She takes a big bite. "Maybe we could write postcards later?" Summer says it through a mouthful of taco. Shredded cabbage falls from her mouth.

"To who?"

She takes a drink of horchata and gives me a crazy look over the glass. "Friends? Family?" She says it like it's obvious. Then she holds me in her gaze. I grow more and more uncomfortable.

"I've kinda only been hanging around one girl."

Summer stirs her horchata with her straw. "Oh?"

"Fern."

"Oh. Right."

"And then my mom made me stop seeing her."

"Why?"

My eyes get small. "My mom used to love Fern, because she never had to worry when I was with her. But then suddenly she decided Fern was bad for me. That she was controlling me, and keeping me from growing."

Summer nods. She opens her mouth and moves the taco toward it. But then she pauses, and holds the taco steady. "Am *I* controlling you? Making you do things you don't want to do?"

My eyes are their right size again as I watch her watching me, waiting for my answer. I scoop some guacamole onto a chip and stuff it into my mouth to give myself time to think of my response.

It's like Fern *enjoys* feeling scared and spooked. She loves spooky books and scary movies, and anything creepy. But I think maybe I only pretended to be scared because I was hanging around her. That's how it feels right now, but it also feels like a big mess I can't understand or find my way out of.

Summer isn't so complicated. I think of the list of

goals in the drawer. Mom's goals for me, and my goals. But even though Mom wrote three of the five, now six, all of them are mine now.

Finally I answer. Definitively. "No. You're definitely not controlling me."

"You're sure?"

I nod. "Absolutely."

She grins. "Good."

And neither was Fern, I think to myself. I don't want to say it, though. Not now, anyway. So I take a bite of my veggie taco so I can't.

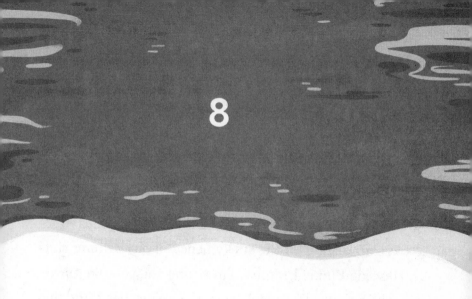

8

SUMMER AND I are in line at Pinkie Promise in the afternoon. Our turn comes, and we are greeted by Otis.

"Dudes! How's the surf?"

Summer holds up her empty hands. "No boards, no waves."

Otis tilts his head back in recognition. "It was pretty tame this morning. But it wouldn't be a bad day for teaching Betty."

I've gotten used to being called Betty, so I don't correct him the way I used to. I kinda like it now, like somehow I'm a different person. A *new* person.

"We'll get her there," Summer says. "We're working our way to it. She threw about a thousand savage punches at a rip current yesterday."

"Well, definitely let me know when you catch your first wave," he says to me. "And it shall rain free ice cream."

Summer laughs. I laugh, but too late. I was slow reacting because I was busy worrying, picturing myself trying to stand on a surfboard.

Moments later we're scarfing down our cups of ice cream, sitting on the sticky bench in our bathing suits outside Pinkie Promise. I'm trying the pancake flavor, which tastes like maple syrup. Summer has mint chip with her usual mountain of whipped cream. This side of Main Street is in the afternoon shade, which means we don't have to eat it in a hurry before the sun melts it.

"You've conquered the ankle busters," Summer says between bites. "You've swum against a gnarly rip current. Bigger and better things tomorrow?"

I nod, though I'm not really sure. Describing it as bigger than swimming against the rip current, which was a terrifying mistake, doesn't make me thrilled to see what she has planned for me next.

"Why is this called a bite of ice cream?" Summer looks at her spoon questioningly. "You don't really bite it, and it's not really a lick since it isn't on a cone."

"Good question."

"Calling it a spoonful doesn't describe what your mouth does to it."

I don't know what to say to that. But I like listening to her talk.

"Maybe a *glop*?" she asks.

"Glop?"

"Yeah, we could call it a glop. Like, 'gimme a glop of that.'"

"I'm in," I say.

Then my phone buzzes. I pick it up and look at the screen.

"*Ugh*. I forgot. I'm supposed to FaceTime with my dad and his girlfriend. He's in Switzerland so I kinda need to get this."

"It's like I'm meeting your family!"

I scoff. "If you wanna call him that."

I lick my lips clean and push my hair out of my face. Then I tap the screen to connect. "Hey, Dad."

"*Bonjour*, Juillet!" He's smiling, looking ridiculous in a white dinner jacket. "We're just finishing up at a bistro here in Zurich. Say hello to Genevieve while I pay the check!" He hands the phone to his girlfriend. She appears on-screen, arranging herself so I can also see her fabulous dress and glass of champagne. She's wearing sunglasses, as always, though it's nighttime there.

"Hello, Genevieve."

"Hallo, Juillet." She's got this mysterious, fake

European accent. She's actually originally from Mobile, Alabama. "You look like you've been kissed by flames."

I glance to Summer, who's got this smile of amused disbelief. But I won't smile.

"I've been in the sun. Learning to surf."

Genevieve scoffs. "Surf? You? Aren't you afraid of jellyfish?"

Summer grabs the phone and turns it toward herself. "There's no jellyfish in Dogtown. Just sharks."

I push Summer away and turn the screen back to my face.

Genevieve frowns. "Who was that? Do they not have hairbrushes in this dog town?"

I frown back at her. "That's Summer. She's my friend."

"Well, since you've become so brave as to surf, you must come with your father and me when we go skiing in the Alps this winter! And I know a wonderful hair salon to fix you and your friend."

"I'll probably ski this winter, but I'm gonna do it somewhere else." Total lie.

"In California!" Summer says, bumping her face back into the frame.

Dad reappears and takes the phone from Genevieve. I'm *so* mad at him, so I hand mine to Summer. She moves her shades from her hair to her eyes.

"Hello?" He squints, looking slightly confused. "Juillet?"

"Yeah! Hey, Dad!" Summer grins at him.

He furrows his brow. "Look, our taxi is here and we're about to see a show. I'll give you a shout as soon as I can. Say hello to your mother for me, okay?"

"Sure thing, Pops! Give my kisses to Genevieve. And send me some Swiss chocolate!" Summer practically shouts it, then taps the screen to disconnect.

She moves the shades back to her hair and turns to me with a goofy smile, then covers her mouth like maybe she did something wrong. I cover my mouth too, and we both start laughing. We laugh so hard tears come, which is convenient, 'cause I'm pretty sure I was gonna cry anyway.

Finally we calm down. My tears dry in the breeze. Zurich melts away, the man who ruined my life melts away, and we're back to the bench in front of Pinkie Promise in Ocean Park, eating our ice cream before *it* melts away.

I'm thinking that the pancake ice cream was a good choice, that I'll have to experiment with new flavors more often. "I've never actually been skiing," I say. "And I know I told Genevieve I was learning to surf, but I haven't made my mind up about it yet. Okay?"

Summer nods, dips back into her mint chip.

I look into my almost-empty cup, and dig a spoon-ful. I think of Genevieve and her stupid face. "Maybe I'll try boogie boarding tomorrow."

Summer doesn't say anything, but out of the cor-ner of my eye I can see a little smile. Then she scoots across the sticky bench until her bare leg is against mine.

At night I lie in bed, doing research on boogie board-ing on my phone. Clearly, the advantage of being on a boogie board is that if a tsunami were to come, at least I'd be on something that floats. Unfortunately, I learn that the biggest drawback, according to a web search of *how to die while boogie boarding*, is that when you lie on a boogie board with your arms and legs sticking out, you apparently look very much like a sea turtle or a sea lion, at least to any dim-witted sharks that might be lurking beneath. The important fact here being that sea turtles and sea lions are two of sharks' favorite foods.

I'm trying to talk myself into the possibility that Summer will forget about boogie boarding entirely, but I can't even get myself to believe that, since she's pretty much always in a swimsuit. She's always look-ing for an excuse to get in the water. So I think about possible fake injuries or medical conditions that would prevent me from being able to go in the water. Unfortunately, all I can come up with are jimmy leg and scrivener's palsy.

I threw away the list of goals twice, but I also pulled it out of the garbage twice. And now it haunts me, telling me I really want to do the things written on it.

And I believe it because it's true. I really *do* want to do the things on the list.

I can do that. I can ride a stinking boogie board.

Or I can die trying.

9

THE FOLLOWING MORNING I'm ignoring alien orders when Summer comes up the sidewalk, a boogie board under each arm. One for her, one for me. She also has a big smile.

"Ta-da!" she says dramatically, handing me my board. "Let's catch some waves on these sponges!"

I smile weakly and examine the board. It stands as high as my ribs, and it's made of a firm, foamy material. There's a black leash with a Velcro cuff to attach to my wrist.

I carry the beach bag over my left shoulder, the boogie board under my right arm, as we take Ocean Park Boulevard down the hill. The ocean is ahead in the distance, stretching all the way to China, to Alaska, to Australia. When I think of the map, the globe, it's also wrapping around the continents and coming back from behind at Florida and New York. It's got me completely surrounded, but I'm marching off to meet it. It'll never suspect that I'm coming right at it, head-on.

Crossing Main Street, I feel like all the people we see can tell it's the first time I've carried a boogie board under my arm. Like I'm an obvious impostor.

But then I think that when I come away from the shore later today, that will no longer be true. The thought becomes a feeling that fills me, carries me.

"Boogie boarding is a great way to learn about waves," Summer says. Our feet hit the sand. "Just like with surfing, you have to catch them in the right spot. But it's easier."

I nod. She's not looking at me, but I nod anyway.

"You have to figure out for yourself how far forward your head will be. Some people like to have it back over the board, some people have it a little bit in front. You can watch and learn from me about catching the waves just right. I don't always get them, and sometimes they get *me* pretty good. But this is gonna be a blast."

We keep walking until our feet are wet. The ocean roars its objections.

She turns to me, smiling. "Are you ready?"

Maybe, just with this particular teacher. *"Yes."*

As the cold water rises above my knees, I think

about the pool where I swim at the country club back home. This is just like it, except here it's saltier and choppier.

And sharks.

Slimy fingers pull at my shins, but it's just seaweed. We press on, and the water rises above my belly button.

"Bounce over the incoming waves!" she shouts over the roar.

"Okay!"

When the waves hit, we jump up and hold our boards against ourselves.

"When you learn to surf, I'll teach you how to duck dive under the rakers."

"Right." That sounds terrifying, but I'm not gonna argue about it just now. After all, it's just water, just like the sink. Just like the bathtub. Except the ocean is somewhat larger. And deeper.

And sharks.

"Now we can kick our way out!" Summer falls onto her board and starts paddling and kicking toward the horizon. I do as she does.

A big wave mashes us, passes beneath us. But we only give up a little ground, or water, and continue pressing away from shore.

Then finally we get to a place where there are no

more big waves. Or, rather, the big waves aren't big yet. We're belly-down on our boards.

Summer looks out toward the open sea, then turns to face the shore. "We're just past the break zone. We watch for a good wave, then paddle in. You want to be going as fast as you can when the wave comes up on you, but you also need to be in the right spot. If you're too far out it rolls beneath you, and if you're too far in it crushes you."

"Okay," I say. But I must not look very encouraged.

"Just think of it like the ocean is a giant car and you're a little bug trying to catch a ride on the windshield. Without being splatted."

I grimace. "I don't think that usually ends very well for the bugs."

"Don't worry," Summer says. "Just watch me and do what I do." She splashes me. "This is gonna be great."

She looks over her shoulder. A small ridge of water swells behind us.

"Not this one."

The wave passes beneath us like an immeasurably large beast, lifting us and then setting us down again.

Summer smiles. "If we were surfing, we couldn't be so close to each other. With surfing you need space to shred. But boogie boarding, you pretty much just launch yourself at the beach."

Another nod from me.

She studies the next wave, watches it being born. "Not this one."

It swells, rolls underneath us, tumbling our boards, tipping us forward. My face gets dunked in the water.

So does Summer's. She spits her hair out of her face. "That might have been a good one. My bad."

I smile. I taste the salt in my nose and on my lips. It probably tastes the same in the Indian Ocean, and in the North Sea. It's all one giant bowl of miso soup.

"Whoa." She looks from the next wave to me, then begins kicking toward shore. "*This*. Catch it!"

I do as she does. I grip the board and kick like a tsunami is chasing me. Then I feel it behind me, the wave, but it doesn't pass beneath me or crush me—instead I stay in front of it on my board, on top of its front edge. We've *got* it, and instantly I understand what this is about, getting a free ride from nature, a joyride, perched on the nose of the ocean like a hood ornament as it crashes into the continent. I feel like a dog with its head out a car window, like a flat stone skipping over a pond. Like a little girl riding her father's shoulders.

I hear Summer whoop, and she's there to my left. She looks at me with wild excitement, like it's *her* first ride, not mine.

The wave carries us onward, bouncing us a couple

of times as we enter shallow water. The waders dodge us as we pass them, small children and a father with a big belly. Finally the wave pulls our boards onto the sand, and quickly draws away to be reborn in the depths.

Summer pushes herself up from her board, from the sand. She gives me a hand and pulls me to my feet.

"Betty! You're a natural!"

"Did I do good?" I ask.

She makes a crazy face, then pushes me away playfully. "That was epic! Nobody does that on their first wave!"

I smile sheepishly.

"Again?" she asks.

"Again," I reply.

The day slips away as we ride and ride. Sometimes we get the waves and sometimes the waves get us, and sometimes nothing really happens. Now the sun is somewhere off to the west, maybe directly over Hawaii. I'm shivering from the cold water, warm from the pink the sun has painted my shoulders in spite of my SPF 144 sunscreen.

"One more?" she finally asks. Apparently even Summer has limits.

"One more," I agree.

"But it needs to be a good one." She turns back

toward the water and begins trudging through it. "The last wave is *always* a good one, 'cause you never leave on a bad wave."

The next wave is the last wave, because it *is* a good one. Not the very best of the day, but not one to make us demand a do-over. Good enough to leave the beach with.

We're silent and exhausted as we walk away from the shore, the sun at our backs. It's like heading up the aisle for the exit in a theater after a really great movie. On the slope in front of us, the houses and trees and buildings of Ocean Park bask in the sun of late afternoon. Then Summer stops in the middle of the wide swath of sand and turns to me.

"Thank you," she says.

"For what?"

Summer raises her arms, gesturing to our surroundings, gathering all of it in. "For sharing this with me. For helping me remember that it's *worth* sharing."

She stands there smiling at me for a moment, and I stand there smiling back. While I try to think of a response, I hear the cry of seagulls carried on the roar of the ocean, smell sunscreen in the beach's bouquet, taste the salt of the sea on my lips. Just when I'm starting to get uncomfortable with so much smiling, such an abundance of happiness, she shakes her head—the *good* kind of shaking her head—and turns back toward North America, toward California and Ocean Park, the snack bar, and an extra-large order of onion rings.

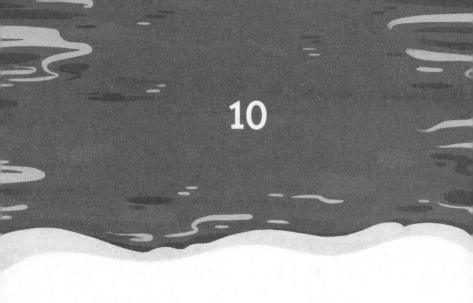

10

THE NEXT DAY is more of the same, only better. By the time Summer and I ignore alien orders at eleven, I'm so amped I forget to worry about Third Street even a little. I charge into the water at Summer's side like I can't wait to meet a shark. We ride and ride until I'm completely noodle-armed from paddling. In the late afternoon I fall asleep in the sun on a beach towel beside Summer, and when I wake up she's smiling at me. She tells me *I* was smiling in my sleep.

We stop by Pinkie Promise after leaving the beach. Otis throws his arms up when he sees us.

"Duuuuudes! Looks like you've been riding something?"

Summer holds up her boogie board. I keep mine under my arm.

"Well, how was it?"

Summer and Otis watch *me*, waiting for my response. I look at my bare feet.

"Amazing." I don't know why I'm so shy about having had a great time.

"Betty is a natural," Summer says.

Otis claps his hands together. "Well, they don't name you Betty unless you were born to ride waves."

This doesn't make any sense, because nobody called me Betty until Otis did on my first day here. But instead of pointing this out, I just smile.

We place our orders—cones, so we can walk home with them while holding our boogie boards. Mint chip for me and butter pecan for Summer.

"Hey, I just had an idea," Otis says as he scoops. "Alert the press." He hands me my cone. "Dude, is Summer teaching you yoga to prepare for your first wave on a surfboard?"

"Yoga?" I ask.

Summer slaps her forehead. "Dude! That is a stellar idea. There's lots of poses that'll be good for balance and strength!"

"Yoga?" I repeat.

"Here!" Otis finishes shaping Summer's cone and hands it to her. "Let me demonstrate!" He comes around the counter and stands with his legs apart.

"This is the warrior pose. This'll help you stay balanced as you serve in Neptune's navy!" I watch as he points his left foot outward, bends into his left knee, and raises his arms, palms down, until they're parallel to the floor. He gazes out past the fingertips of his left hand. "Now you try it!"

Otis holds the pose. It doesn't look like he or Summer will take no for an answer, so I hand my cone to Summer, and do my best to duplicate his stance.

Summer smiles. "That's good! Make sure your knee is directly above your ankle on the left foot. Nice."

"Perfect!" Otis says. "Now get out of the pose by pretending you're pushing your feet farther apart, but *without* pushing them farther apart."

This doesn't make any sense, but it works. I pop back up to standing straight.

Otis has me repeat the pose in the opposite direction. I'm hoping we're done.

"She should learn downward dog, too," Summer says.

"For sure!" Otis agrees.

Downward dog sounds humiliating, and it looks even more so, on my hands and feet with my butt up high in the air. At least Otis is doing it too. His messy blond hair and seashell necklace hang beneath his face as he stares down at the floor. Summer just smiles and alternates licks between her ice cream cone and mine.

"Now bend into your right knee," Otis says. "Now your left. Do you feel your Achilles stretching?"

"Yes."

It gets more embarrassing when a line of customers starts to form. They've got big cameras and tourist brochures sticking out of their pockets. They point at me and comment on the spectacle in foreign languages.

"Namaste, everybody!" Summer tells the people waiting for ice cream. She does the namaste bow with the two ice cream cones held together. "Otis will be right with you. I'm sure there's just a couple more poses he wants to go over. But feel free to join in!"

From the downward dog position, and then the plank position—where I hold myself up like a diving board—I can see the customers smiling. A woman holding a camera with a big lens takes a picture of me and Otis. I guess for them—the tourists—it's all part of the strange attraction of California. I guess it is for me, too.

After the plank pose, Otis jumps to his feet and fist-bumps me. "Awesome, Betty! Keep working on those poses, and Summer can add some others to your practice!"

Summer nods as she hands me my cone. "Heck,

yeah! We'll have you surfing in no time!"

I take a lick of my mint chip. It tastes even better than usual, like my senses have opened up from the yoga, and in this moment catching a wave while standing on my feet seems almost within the realm of possibility. And if I'm willing to pose like a dog in an ice cream shop to make it happen, maybe that means I really *do* want to catch a wave.

Mom comes home early enough to have dinner with me. I'm practicing the warrior pose when she walks in the door.

"You're doing yoga?"

"Summer and Otis taught me some poses. It feels kinda cool."

She puts her laptop bag on the table. "There's a yoga studio in Lakeshore near our home where you can take lessons. If you like."

I pop up out of the pose. "Maybe." I'm thinking that it won't be the same if it's not taught by Otis and Summer. But maybe anyway.

We take a cab to a surf-themed vegan place in downtown Santa Monica. It's called Wave of Mutilation. TVs on every wall show nonstop footage of surfers riding gigantic waves as high as houses. At least the ones in Ocean Park aren't so terrifyingly big.

The food is amazing. For drinks they only serve filtered water, and only at room temperature, with a lemon wedge. But the food is so tasty, I'm on board with whatever they might say about food and drink, and why.

"You've got a healthy appetite," Mom observes. "You must be staying active."

"Yeah." I dip my taco into the ranchero sauce. I spring the question before taking a bite. "Can I have some money for a shorty?"

She smiles. "What exactly is a shorty?"

"It's a wetty for summertime when the water isn't too cold." Her face shows a complete lack of understanding, so I add, "A wet suit."

"Oh." She brightens. "Have you been going in the water?"

"Yes. And boogie boarding."

"Really?"

"Summer is teaching me."

"Wow." I can tell she's trying not to make a big deal of it, but she's happy I'm hanging around someone adventurous. She's probably counting in her head how many fears I'm ignoring to do this.

"If I had a dad, he'd probably be the one to teach me to boogie board. And to help me get through riding the Ferris wheel. But instead I have Summer."

"You do have a dad."

"I do? Oh, right. But he's busy fixing the faces of rich people so they look like mannequins. And running around Europe with a girl who's barely older than me."

Mom starts to say something but doesn't, then reaches for her water and takes a sip.

It makes me mad at myself for being mean-spirited and sarcastic, bringing up the topic of Genevieve, ruining the mood during my time with Mom. But I'm also mad at *Mom* because she didn't get the hint, that if I had a *mom* who ever spent time with me, *she* could be the one. She could be the one to boogie board with me, and everything else that's a little bit scary but super scary when you're alone.

Instead I have Summer.

"Did you FaceTime with your father today?"

"A couple days ago. For like five seconds. Then he handed the phone to Genevieve. Summer and I punked him by having Summer pretend to be me when he got back on the screen. But then he was back to his fabulous new life."

"Well, he is a busy man."

"Busy eating a fancy dinner and taking his doll to a show."

Mom takes another sip of water, then clears her

throat. "Are you deliberately trying to hurt me by reminding me of his choices?"

I slump down in my chair, away from the table. "No. I'm trying to remind you how much it hurts *me*."

Mom takes her wallet from her purse. "So, how much does a shorty cost?"

"I can get a really good one for less than two hundred bucks."

She raises her eyebrows. "That's not cheap."

"But it'll keep me from getting too cold when I'm in the water for a long time. And it'll help keep my sunburn from getting worse."

She puts her wallet away and picks up her fork.

"And it's better for rough conditions. Sometimes the waves tug at my bikini bottom so everyone can see half my butt."

Mom's eyebrows jump as she swallows a bite of food. She reaches for her glass of tepid water to wash it down. "We can stop by an ATM after dinner."

I take a bite of taco to keep from smiling. But it's not a smile at her agreeing to buy me a shorty. More like the unhappy kind of smile that always comes when I try to tell Mom how I'm feeling, and all she can do is throw money at me.

11

THE NEXT MORNING Summer and I ignore alien orders, then walk down the hill to the little library. Later we'll shop for a shorty for me and go boogie boarding after the marine layer burns off. But right now, Summer says overcast skies are the best time for books. We've got our swimsuits on, just because.

"There's a bigger library in downtown Santa Monica that I can take you to next time we go there," Summer says. She opens the door and holds it for me. "But this one is cute and it's really well stocked for being so small."

She walks in like she owns the place, and waves at a librarian—a man wearing a striped sweater—who waves back at her. I'm worried that Summer is drawing attention to how little we're wearing in this place, which is, after all, a public library. I lean to her and speak in a whisper. "Is it okay that we're wearing bathing suits?"

She gives me a look like I'm kooky. Apparently all my questions are kooky. "Of course! This is *Dogtown*."

I'm pretty sure if I ask about whether it's okay that our feet are bare, the answer will be the same.

The library's shelves are low. Its windows are high. Summer leads me to the kids' area.

"Why is it called Dogtown?"

Summer kneels low in front of one of the shelves. "Because tons of people walk their dogs on Main Street. Which makes it tricky for skateboarders."

I think about this, and imagine a skateboard having a collision with a Chihuahua. Then I picture a skateboarder tripping over a border collie's leash, or ramming into a mastiff. I shudder.

"They pretty much get all the new titles here," Summer says, running her fingertips across the spines of books. "But the very best book is an *old* one." Her fingers go from left to right on the lowest shelf, then stop, and go back to the left. She frowns. "*Dang*. Someone must have checked it out. Remind me to show you my own copy at my house."

"What book are you looking for?"

"*The Perfect Wave*. I've read it like a million times.

I'm sure you can guess what it's about."

I smile.

We spend half an hour searching the shelves for books, sharing our finds, sampling them. Then we carry our selections to the front desk.

The librarian in the striped sweater greets us. "Did you girls find some good books to check out?"

"Yes!" Summer says. "Though my new friend here seems to be reading her way to a darker future."

I frown, then look at the titles I've selected, spread out on the counter.

Zombies Slurped My Eye Sockets at Dawn.

Game Show of the Apocalypse.

Eat or Be Eaten.

"Everything isn't always all cheerful," I say in my own defense. "Bad things happen."

The librarian's smile disappears. He looks at Summer, then gathers the books and turns to scan them.

"I *know*," Summer says, sounding annoyed. "But bad things don't *always* happen."

A dreadful feeling hangs in the air. Finally the librarian turns back to us and addresses Summer. "Do you have your library card, dear?"

Summer grins, then reaches to the back of her bikini bottom with both hands. "Hmm. No pockets there." That quickly, the feeling of dread has disappeared.

Like the sun burning off the morning clouds, Summer shines through.

The librarian returns Summer's smile and pushes the pile of books to her. "I can just get the number from your file."

Summer leans across the counter. "Thank you, Joe! You're a prince." She divides the stack of books between us, and we say good-bye to Joe the librarian.

"We're all thinking about your brother," he says.

Summer nods and says nothing. But her smile has disappeared.

We head out the door. The marine layer has burned off, and the sun shines brightly.

"You have a brother?" I ask as we walk up the hill, to her home and my cottage. "Is that who Hank is?" Again she nods and says nothing, but it's like the sun has gone back behind the clouds. I look up, and the sky is bright blue, but it *feels* like the sun is back behind the clouds.

As we walk in silence, I wonder about Summer. I try to figure this girl out. Always sunny, except when a cloud passes over her, a cloud she won't speak of.

Maybe by the end of July she'll let me know her completely.

12

IT'S LATE MORNING on one of Mom's rare days off.
I've got on one of my pairs of dark blue jeans, but not
to wear—they're about to become a pair of cutoffs.
Scissors found in a drawer are lying on the big table in
the front room, and Mom is kneeling before me with
a white china marker. She presses the tip high on one
leg and makes a mark.

"Higher," I say.

I watch as she moves the tip up—but barely at all—
and makes another mark.

"Higher," I repeat.

She looks up at me. "Why don't you show me how
high you've got in mind?"

I reach around to the back of my leg and feel for a
good location. "Here."

She tsks. "I don't want you walking around with your butt on display."

I scowl. "My butt won't be on display. Just my legs."

Mom sighs, then moves the tip up and makes the mark. "Well, you do have beautiful legs."

"Really?"

"*Yes*," she says definitively. She marks the other leg, then stands back and smiles.

I drop the jeans and lay them across the big table in the front room, then grab the shears. A quick *snip-snip*, *snip-snip*, and then I pull the threads apart to fray them so it looks like I've been wearing them since school got out. Now I've got cutoffs just like Summer's.

An hour later I'm wearing them, walking out the door to go to Main Street with Mom at lunchtime. It's day thirteen of my holiday, and Summer said she is busy until later in the afternoon with some family stuff, which she offered zero details of. This works out okay, because today is a day away from saving lives at the hospital for Mom, so she and I are hanging out. I'm kinda excited to be showing her the town I've gotten to know.

Mom looks not too overwhelmingly uncool in her bathing suit and wrap as we head down the hill on Ocean Park Boulevard. I'm wearing a bikini top and my newly fashioned cutoffs, flip-flops, and dark sunglasses with bright green frames. Also practically a whole tube of sunscreen.

"Show me the way," Mom says happily. "I'm so proud of you for learning to find your bearings in the neighborhood."

We walk on Ocean Park Boulevard, down the hill, just like Summer and I have been doing.

"Look up at those blossoms!" I point to the tall stalks above us, like I'm the first to discover them. "Have you ever seen so many hummingbirds at once?"

"Wow!" Mom smiles, but I know she's thinking about Third Street just ahead, and wondering how she's gonna get me through it. She takes my hand. "So . . ."

"Look over there!" I say. Mom wants to distract me, but I'll do it for her. "That's the Ferris wheel at the pier! Me and Summer rode it at sunset. We should go there after lunch!"

"Okay!"

"And beyond, in the distance, those are the Santa Monica Mountains. They get purple when the sun goes down. Summer says there are mountain lions living there."

"Really?"

"Yeah!"

We arrive at Main Street. "Pinkie Promise is that

way. Remember how we went there on our first night in town?"

"I do."

"We can go there at the end of the day. Summer and I have been there together. Lots of times."

As we walk down Main Street, I look at the reflection of my legs every chance I get, but I try to make it not too obvious. There's always something I might be looking at in the storefront windows, like shoes and purses and a dog lying at its owner's feet in a coffee shop, but also my legs looking not too dreadfully skinny or pale. Maybe not as athletic as Summer's legs, but looking at least like they've been taken out and used every now and then. Especially recently.

We arrive at the taco shop, its tables spilling onto the sidewalk.

"This is it!" I say. "Do you wanna eat outside?"

"Of course!" Mom says. "It's too beautiful not to."

The host seats us under an umbrella on the front patio. Mom studies the menu. I know what I want but I pretend to look at it too. But I guess I'm really looking at Mom.

"Squid tacos?" She smirks. "I think I'll pass on that, thank you."

"The veggie tacos have avocado. They're so good! That's what Summer and I had."

She smiles and puts her menu aside. "Then that's what I'll have."

We give our orders to the server. I sip my lemon water while Mom gazes across the table at me, looking happy. A breeze moves through her hair, and she turns to face it.

I feel a buzz in my back pocket. I try to ignore it.

"Are you gonna check it?" Mom asks.

"I already know who it is. It's gonna be another sad text from Fern."

Mom stares at me. Obviously neither one of us can say anything about anything else until I check it. I pull the phone from my back pocket.

Remember how we used to debate whether it was me or you a boy was checking out? I think the boys must have always been looking at you. Because now when I'm alone at the mall or at the pool I'm totally invisible.

Just like that I feel terrible. And I *deserve* to feel terrible. I stuff the phone back into my pocket.

"When are you gonna let me see Fern again?"

That pretty much wipes the smile from Mom's face.

"Well, do you think that's a good idea? Being boxed up at a mall and refusing to see your other friends, or make new friends, or do the things that used to be important to you?"

I frown. "I don't have any other friends. Not at home, anyway."

"Of course you do. You just need to reach out. And stop refusing them."

A tray of food goes by to another table.

"What if it wasn't Fern's fault?" I ask. "What if it was all *my* fault?"

She clears her throat. "I do think it's good for you to acknowledge your part in it."

"But the—"

Her phone buzzes on the table, interrupting. She glances at a text message without reaching for it, and smiles at me.

She crosses her legs.

I look at her, then at her phone. I watch as she uncrosses her legs.

I begin again. "The day I missed the piano recital—"

Her phone rings this time. She leans forward and picks it up. She says, "Yes, yes, yes. Of course." Then she puts her phone down.

I turn away to the view across the street. It's nothing—it's a liquor store or a little market.

I feel Mom's hand reach to mine.

"I'm so sorry, Juillet. Duty calls."

I'm not gonna turn toward her. Especially if my

eyes are suddenly wet.

"I hate to do this. To leave you." Her hand withdraws. "Do you mind?"

She knows I mind and that she's gonna go whether I like it or not. So I don't bother answering.

"I'm so sorry, Juillet." She fishes in her purse. "Here's some money. You can stay and eat the delicious tacos and do whatever you'd like. And please bring my order back to the cottage. You know the way back, right? Of course you do—you brought me here." She waits in vain for me to respond, or to look at her. "I'll see you tonight, okay?"

Her chair legs drag on the cement as she rises and hurries away. I count to ten before turning to watch her go, then glance at the hundred-dollar bill on the table, pinned beneath my water glass.

Money is never the problem. Hundred-dollar bills are always present.

So it's another date with Mom cut short.

I lean away from the table and look down at my *jeans* cut short. I wonder what Summer will think of them.

My day gets better when Summer knocks on the door of our cottage a couple of hours later, and takes me to the beach. After chowing down on veggie burgers and sweet potato fries at the snack bar, she and I are lying on towels near the water's edge. But even if we weren't beached from the feast, there'd be no boogie boarding today. Summer says it would be a waste of time with the waves so choppy from the wind. We're wearing our bathing suits just so we can get our gills wet.

Summer turns over onto her stomach. "Spray me?"

The sun is getting lower over the Pacific. It's beginning to make everything look golden. But it's still high enough to require sunscreen.

I take the can of sunscreen out of the canvas bag and shake it, then direct it up and down her legs, her back, her arms and shoulders.

Her right hand reaches back to a spot on her hip. "Can you spray extra right here?"

I lean in and look at the area she's indicated. I give another layer to her lower back, right side, just above her bikini bottom, where a series of nearly white marks arcs toward her side, like a dotted line. The sunscreen makes the tiny golden hairs on her skin get shinier.

"What are these marks?" I ask.

She takes a moment to answer. "It's a scar. The sunscreen keeps it from getting worse."

Sitting above her, I study the line of marks on her back, emerging from her swimsuit bottom, curling toward her waist.

"How'd you get it?"

Again she doesn't answer right away. I'm starting to worry that her reluctance has something to do with the secrecy surrounding her home life.

"Men in gray suits" comes her facedown, towel-muffled reply.

"Huh?"

Another delay. Then, "Shark."

I draw away quickly and fall to the sand.

"A shark?"

She rolls over and sits up. "A very small shark. Barely bigger than me. And he just gave me a nibble. He bit my butt and said *no thanks.*"

"He bit your butt?"

"I barely even bled. Sharks like to eat fat things like sea lions. But I'm lean. See?" She jumps to her feet and strikes a pose. "And so are you. And all humans, really, compared to sea lions. So don't worry about it."

"So they have to bite you to figure out whether they want to eat all of you?"

"It wasn't even here." She drops back to the towel. "It was up by San Francisco. It's much more sharky up there. And down here we have the Big Kahuna to protect us. One time he punched a shark right in the nose. Did you know that?" She searches my expression. "Of course you didn't know. But he *did.* A whole line of surfers saw it. Scared it right out of the bay."

I frown. "You're acting like it's no big deal."

"Are you kidding? It sucked! He ruined my favorite board. And my mom wouldn't let me back in the water for practically a week."

I stare at her, then look off at the ocean, watching for dorsal fins. I don't know why I'm letting Summer drag me into her life of danger. Then I smile, a small smile, because I know that the next time the waves are decent, I'll be back out there with her.

13

EARLY SATURDAY MORNING, Summer and I are standing by one of the lifeguard shacks with a group of mostly ancient people wearing matching aqua-blue T-shirts. She talked me into helping this group—the Beachcombers—pick up garbage on the sand. Where I come from they make prisoners pick up garbage, but maybe there aren't enough prisoners here.

The apparent leader of the group—an old guy with a backpack of supplies—hands me an aqua-blue shirt of my very own. I smile grimly.

"Put it on!" Summer says excitedly.

It's more the sort of color my mom would choose for me. Plus it's got the words *Beachcombers—Keepin' It Clean!*

"This isn't exactly a cool shirt," I say.

"Yes it is! You just don't know it yet."

Instead of rolling my eyes, I pull the aqua-blue shirt over the black one I'm wearing, which in turn covers my swimsuit top.

Then the old guy with the backpack raises a megaphone to his mouth and speaks. There's something wrong with the megaphone, or how he's using it, so instead of hearing him speak we get a series of excruciatingly loud screeches while everyone around covers their ears. After a few very long seconds he lowers the megaphone and smiles.

Summer uncovers her ears and turns to me. "Basically he said we're gonna fan out across the beach and make our way north at the plodding pace kept by Gladys over there." Summer points to a woman in a bikini who looks about a hundred and ten years old, with stringy hair and a walker. "We'll pick up all the trash we see between here and the pier, and if our bags get full or our latex gloves rip, we can get new supplies from him. Also, you and me get to be at the water's edge since first-timers get dibs on seashells. And you're a first-timer." She smiles.

"Is that why you're making me do this? So you can get dibs on seashells?"

"No! This is about paying our respects to the ocean, and the surf gods. This is just part of the deal."

"Okay."

I follow her down to the wet sand, and we form a line with the other blue shirts that extends all the distant way to where the beach meets the grass of the park. There are a few dozen of us, spaced ten feet apart. But Summer and I stay closer than that.

The megaphone makes another unpleasant screech, sending seagulls scattering, and the beachcombing begins like a race nobody wants to win.

Summer smiles at me, then kicks at a wave that rolls across our ankles.

"How often do you do this?" I ask.

"Every two weeks. There are other groups too. Like the Crabby Scavengers."

I reach down for a plastic bottle cap that's dancing with the tide. "It seems pointless."

Summer stops. "What do you mean?"

I drop the bottle cap into my bag. "People keep on littering."

She begins walking again. "And we keep picking it up."

This makes very little sense to me, like she's choosing to be on the wrong side of a miserable equation.

"And," she says, bending for a seashell, which she examines and discards, "not all of the garbage is because of litterbugs. Seagulls pick it out of the metal cans and scatter it. The wind carries it. And anyway, it doesn't seem pointless when you're picking it up. It doesn't seem like a problem that can't be solved. It feels like a problem that you *are* solving, right then. With every piece you pick up."

I reach for a broken toy shovel and drop it in my bag.

Then Summer gasps, and throws her bag to the dry sand. She pulls off her latex gloves, bends down with her hands cupped together to scoop at the sand where the water has just drawn away.

I get closer to see, and I hear her speaking quietly, words I can't make out, like she's soothing a baby.

She picks something from her wet handfuls, then drops the sand away and lays what she's found on her palm. She turns and stands, holding it to me.

"Look!"

I do. It's the tiniest sand dollar ever. More like a sand dime. I've seen sand dollars in collections and at the lobster restaurant back home, but they were closer to pancake-size.

"So pretty," I say.

"For you."

I look at her eyes. "Really?"

"This is so delicate it can't share my bag with any other shells." She unzips a small cloth bag hanging against her hip. "And don't bump into me!"

We make our way down the beach, all the way to the pier. Even though Gladys with her walker did her best, she dropped out a ways back. But most everyone else kept up and filled their bags with trash. We hand them in to another old guy, who does the namaste bow to us with his hands held together like a prayer. Even the old people do the namaste thing here. I guess they were probably the first ones doing it.

"See you in two weeks!" Summer tells him cheerfully.

We drink a lemonade on the pier and rest for a while, watching the sand fill up with people.

"We've paid our respects to the beach," she says. "We've paid our dues."

I'm too tired from the walk to add much. More the bending down and standing up than the walk. But I feel good, like Summer said I would. Like I really *did* do something useful.

Then Summer says it's time to go. "We have to go back the way we came!"

"Can't we take the bus?"

"We have to see the work we've done!" She takes me by the hand, and we go down the steps from the pier, onto the sand, and back to the south. "Look for garbage!"

I do. There isn't any.

"Keep looking!" she says. "First one to find some gets to pick it up!"

I see an aluminum can standing in the sand, but a guy stretched out on a blanket reaches for it and takes a drink from it.

We walk and walk, and while the beach is filling up with people, there's no garbage. It's my first-ever look at a beach that's spotless.

Finally, halfway back, Summer spots something. She bends down and picks up a cigarette butt, frowning at it. "One time I walked all the way back without seeing anything. This was probably buried in the sand and someone kicked it up."

Then a potato-chip bag drifts by in the breeze. Summer chases it and steps on it, picks it up, then puts the cigarette butt in the potato-chip bag and keeps walking.

It makes me feel sad and a little crazy. We just walked with dozens of people, scouring the beach, and already it's getting littered again.

But then I remember that in two weeks, Summer and the people in aqua-blue shirts will be back at it, cleaning the beach. I decide in this moment that I'll be with them. Because I've bought into this—this girl and her beach, her waves. What this place has given me, and what it promises to give me . . . I've got a feeling it's something I need to give back.

In the evening I'm sitting at the big table in the front room eating strawberries with whipped cream. It's my dinner, more or less, though I've been eating all day. Walking and running all over this town makes me constantly hungry. I've got the can of whipped cream turned upside down, reloading the strawberries, when I hear a knock. I turn and see Summer's face entering the room through the dark window beside the door.

"Hey! Can I have some of that?"

As I recall, I asked her not to surprise me by having her head suddenly appear in the window, but at least this time she knocked first. And I suppose it's become more difficult to scare me. So I smile as I rise from my chair and walk over to the window with the can of whipped cream, shaking it as I go. She opens her mouth and tilts her head. I turn the can over, press the nozzle, and fill her mouth. She swallows.

"Yumzers. Hey, there's a party at the Big Kahuna's. Wanna go?"

"What kind of party?"

"*You* know. A party party. Potato chips sittin' there. Guitars playin'."

I put the cap on the whipped cream. "What kind of people?"

"Neighborhood people. Surfer people."

She tilts her head again. I take the cap back off and fill her mouth with the last of the whipped cream.

"What will people be wearing?"

Summer points at me. "That. But they won't look as good as you do."

I glance down at myself, in part to break my eye contact with Summer. I'm wearing a hoodie that identifies me as a lifeguard for the People's Republic of Santa Monica. Below it are my new cutoffs.

"Don't worry," Summer says, "the actual lifeguards at the party won't think you're uncool for wearing a lifeguard hoodie."

I open my mouth to say something, but nothing comes out.

"Come on!" she says. "Before the guacamole disappears. The Big Kahuna makes guac almost as well as he shreds."

I come outside and join her in the cool night air. She's still wearing the Beachcombers tee, but she's put on a long-sleeved plaid shirt over it, buttoned halfway. She has cutoffs too, but I keep myself from smiling about that, about us being matchers. She grabs my hand and pulls me down the sidewalk, then across the street.

The Big Kahuna's house is a light blue California bungalow with lots of windows. Music spills into the small yard, and the covered front porch is littered with sandals and shoes.

"Bare feet," Summer says. "House rule."

We kick our sandals off and park them to the right of the door. Summer guides me through the open doorway, to a big living room filled with people but not crowded. There's a tall guy playing surf music on an electric guitar plugged into a tiny, fuzzy-sounding amp. There's not a stick of furniture except a table with a few bowls of potato chips and tortilla chips, and guacamole and salsa. Summer pulls me to the guacamole and starts chowing down. Between bites she smiles and waves at various guests, who seem to be of every age, from schoolkids to gray-haired. There's a lady who looks like she's eighty dancing with a boy who could be her great-grandson. People in shorts and dresses and T-shirts and hoodies, long hair and short hair and bald, and wearing hats.

"This guac was definitely made by the man himself." Summer reaches for another tortilla chip. "It's got diced cucumbers in it so it's extra juicy."

I take a chip and scoop up some of the guacamole. It's as unbelievable as Summer says. There's nothing like it in Lakeshore.

"Which one is the Big Kahuna?"

Summer quickly scans the room. "I don't see him. He's probably asleep. But those are his sticks." She points to several surfboards of various sizes standing against the wall.

"Why would he sleep through his own party?"

Summer shrugs. "I'm sure he had a good time. But he likes to wake up early for dawn patrol."

"And he lets people just hang out in his house? What if someone wanted to steal his stuff?"

Summer laughs. "The only things he has of value are his boards. But nobody would take them. That would be totally uncool."

The guitar player begins an old song I recognize, called "Louie Louie." A guy sitting on the floor joins in on a bongo drum. I watch as half the people in the room start dancing. Then I feel a tug on my arm as Summer drags me away from the guacamole table. She pulls me to the middle of the room and begins dancing. Or, rather, she's been dancing the whole way, but when we arrive at the middle of the room she's dancing with *me*.

She shouts the words to the song, about someone named Louie who apparently needs to leave. Summer is grinning, arms high in the air, shaking her head from side to side, golden hair playing on her shoulders.

Her hips move from left to right. She looks totally careless, carefree, like she was born into this, born *for* this. Meanwhile I can feel myself moving, but more like someone walking up stairs or crushing grapes.

Summer doesn't seem to notice how badly I'm dancing. She's laughing and having the best time, like all you have to do is tell her it's a party, give her some guacamole, play a song she likes, and she'll dance like she can't help herself. She looks like she's stumbled upon the edge of happiness, the very limits, without even trying.

She lowers the hand that was celebrating its possession of a guac-dipped tortilla chip, and brings it to her mouth, not missing a beat, moving her face closer to mine while she shakes like a dashboard figure on a bumpy road.

I start laughing and realize I've forgotten how I'm dancing, and discover I'm not dancing so badly, like my body is dancing *me*, and I keep on laughing, and dancing. I've never danced like this in Michigan. Not at my old school, where I had friends, or my new school, where I have just one friend. Back home I only dance because I feel like I have to, but it's never made me feel happy, or free.

Summer puts her hands back above her head and turns until her hip is bumping against mine. I mimic her without thinking or trying. I feel my face shining, my skin glowing.

Then my hip misses hers, and I look down and see she's stopped moving, arms hanging at her sides. I follow her unhappy gaze across the room to the two skater boys who've just entered, the two jerks we saw on the Fourth of July. As they cross the room to where we stand, the taller one smirks and does an imitation of Summer, of how she was dancing, of how *we* were dancing. His sidekick laughs.

Summer folds her arms. "Why don't you skate off a cliff, Wade?"

Wade throws back his head, laughing. "Why don't you feed a landlord, Summer?" His sidekick snorts.

"This party is for cool people," Summer replies.

"So why are you here?" Wade fires back.

The song plays on, but Summer takes my hand and pulls me away from Wade and his friend, out of the living room, down a short wood-floored hall, and into a bathroom. She shuts the door behind us and drops onto the toilet, where she sits, inconsolable.

"Why did they have to come? All the parties in Ocean Park and they had to come to this one."

Beside Summer is a shelf displaying scattered seashells. There's a small watercolor painting of a surfboard above the toilet.

"What did he mean by telling you to feed a land-lord?"

She scoffs. "*Landlord* is surferspeak for a great white shark. You don't really see them here. And if he ever went in the water he'd know that."

I look at my fingernail but don't bite it. "Back on the Fourth of July you said school was tricky. What did you mean?"

Summer stares at the wood planks of the floor. "I kinda told everyone at school to kiss off. Including Wade. Then I stopped going there."

"You stopped going to school? Just like that?"

She shakes her head. "First I got miserable. *Then* I told everyone to kiss off. Now I'm homeschooled."

"Really?"

"No. But that's the story. I mainly stay home and . . . take care of things. My mom doesn't have near enough time to teach me, or enough money to pay someone. She manages just enough to keep the State of California out of our hair." She reaches forward and spins the toilet-paper roll. "It's only been a year. So far."

I'm wondering what could possibly make this girl so unhappy, and whether she'll one day tell *me* to kiss off. But before I can ask, she stands and pushes her hair behind her ears.

"Come on. Let's get out of here."

I follow Summer out of the bathroom. She stops and looks down at a pair of huarache sandals outside a closed door in the hall, then slides her feet inside them, closes her eyes briefly, and steps backs out. "The Big Kahuna's sandals," she whispers. "Step into them for good surf mojo." She points to the sandals and I do the same, stepping my bare feet into them. They're way too big, but they feel comfortably worn. I step back out. Summer nods and I follow her into the living room. She veers toward the wall where the Big Kahuna's boards are standing and touches each one, trailing her fingertips across their surfaces. I follow behind, doing the same, each of the four a different sensation, a record of their births, their heroics, the baking sun and salty sea. Only after we pass the guacamole and head toward the front door do I realize that she wanted to leave not the bathroom but the party. I bend to pick up both pairs of sandals on the porch, 'cause Summer passes them by. I hurry to catch up to her as she crosses the street, then pauses on the sidewalk on the other side. Her house is to the left, my cottage is to the right. She turns to me.

"I'll walk you home," she says.

"Okay."

She's quiet as we travel the few dozen slow steps to the hedge, the front door. Then she turns to me.

"Sorry for ruining it."

I shake my head. "You didn't ruin anything."

"We walked from stellar guac. We bailed on a great song. Both my fault."

"It was those guys' fault," I say.

She looks at her feet, shakes her head. "I don't know. Maybe not."

"It's okay. I'm kinda tired anyway." It's not really true, but I say it.

I'm still holding both pairs of sandals. I'm thinking of bringing this fact up when she steps toward me and puts her arms around me, over my shoulders, and moves close to hug me. As she draws back and turns away from me I realize I never put my arms around *her.* I don't know why I didn't—maybe because of the two pairs of sandals held in my hands—and I don't know why it fills me with a sense of panic that I didn't.

I can't even say good-bye or call out that I still have her sandals as she walks past the hedge and onto the sidewalk. But as I stand there alone in the cool night air, listening to crickets and a song by Buddy Holly from the party across the street, I decide it's okay. Because only the best kind of friends can say good night without saying good night, knowing for certain that they'll be together again at the same spot on the same sidewalk the very next day.

14

THE NEXT DAY we're floating out on the water, just past the impact zone. The sun is warm, the wind is light. It's pretty chill out here on our boogie boards.

Summer glances out to the open water. We're not catching waves at the moment, but she's watching anyway. "So, do you think you'll ever hang out with Fern again?"

"I don't know." That's what I say, but what I *feel* is that I've been a terrible friend to Fern, that I betrayed her, that I don't deserve her.

"Do you think you can find a way to not let her control you?"

I hesitate. "She's not really so bad."

Summer furrows her brow. "Didn't you say she kept

you fearful? Didn't you do all that stuff, the Mistress Snuffles—"

"Scarfia!"

"—because that was what Fern liked to do?"

I frown. "How is that any different than me only doing crazy dangerous things because I'm hanging around you and it's what *you* like to do?" I regret it as soon as I say it.

"Is that how it feels for you?" Summer looks at me with an unfamiliar seriousness. "Am I forcing you to do things you don't want to do?"

I never can say what I need to say, but it's easy to say things I regret. Like the lie I told Mom. The lie about Fern.

"Because we could find a mall somewhere," Summer says. "And maybe there'll be a Salty's Pretzel Shop there."

"Softee's." I smile in spite of myself. "No. I don't want to go to the mall."

"You sure?"

I sigh. "I have a list of goals in a drawer at our cottage. Goals of things to do while I'm here. None of them can be found at the mall. And pretty much all of them are things I couldn't do without you."

Summer smiles. "I'm sure you're wrong about that. I'm sure you could do whatever you set your mind to.

But I'm so glad to be along for the ride."

I smile.

"So, what's on the list?"

I gesture to the open sea. "This."

A wave rolls under us. We rise and fall.

"It just so happens that it's on my list, too." Summer looks back out to sea. Her eyes get big. "Bluebird!"

I look but there's no bird, blue or otherwise. There *is* a wave, though, and Summer turns her boogie board to face the beach and starts paddling. I do the same.

The wave is big, and as we frantically paddle and kick, it picks us up and pushes us in front of it. We've caught it perfectly, and within a few seconds it's clear that it's the best wave of the day, the best wave *ever*. Summer and I are almost close enough to hold hands, and I look at her and she looks at me, laughing, whooping, and we ride and ride, past the boogie boarders who are too close to shore to catch this beast, until we're steering around the waders and are finally deposited on the sand as the wave retreats.

"That was awesome!" Summer shouts, getting to her feet. I unstick myself from the sand, which has a way of feeling like a suction cup. Summer jumps to me and gives me a hug. "That was the longest ride ever. Did you love it?"

"I loved it."

"Another one?"

"Another one."

We take our boards in both hands and skip off into the sea, bouncing over the incoming waves. We relive in words the ride we just took, then we're deeper and paddling out to the same spot. We turn to face the shore.

Summer watches a wave pass beneath us, then paddles backward to go farther out. "That wave we just caught was what's called a bluebird. It's a wave that breaks farther out than the rest. That was why it was bigger, and longer, and more fun. We were lucky to get it."

"Do you think we can get another?" I ask.

"Maybe. Bluebirds are rare. They're something unexpected that comes along and gives you the best time ever. If it doesn't crush you. We can wait out here for a while, and at the very least we can let the waves program us."

I give her a blank look.

"That's what I call the feeling you get from being out in the water all day," she says. "The way you feel like you're rocking back and forth all night long. Have you ever felt that before?"

"Only this week."

She smiles. I smile back. Then I look to the open

water for bluebirds and my heart stutters, my breath catches. I cannot speak, cannot form words, because my eyes are fixed on a group of dorsal fins. Desperately I reach for Summer, but she is too far, and my hand splashes in futility. I cannot breathe, my terror is so complete.

"What?" Summer paddles toward me, reaches for me. The dorsal fins are as close as if they were on my street back home, appearing and reappearing, above and below the surface, moving parallel to the beach. Getting closer.

But Summer follows my gaze, and her eyes light up. "Friends!" she shouts. "Dolphins!"

In rapid succession three—no, four—smooth gray curves break the surface of the water. The dolphins' backs shine as their dorsal fins point to the sky, then cut back into the sea. Now my heart is *racing*. It's soaring. They're so close we can hear the water as they rip through it.

Then a fountain spouts from the surface as one of them leaps into the air. I swear it's smiling at me, at us, as its full glossy length shimmers in the sun. It does a tight turn midair and drops back nose first into the water, tail curling to send an arc of spray at us. It splashes me right in my face.

"Hotdogger!" Summer shouts. "Show-off!"

I'm laughing and crying at the same time, 'cause I went from so scared to so happy, so quickly. We watch the dolphins' fins disappear and appear again as they race away to the south.

"Bluebird!" Summer shouts.

This time I know not to look for a bird, but I do look over my shoulder as I point my board to the shore and begin paddling, paddling. It's the same wave, maybe bigger, and when it reaches us it almost crushes us, tipping my face down into the sea. But after getting a nose full of salt water I'm still riding it, and so is Summer, beside me. We've been worked, we cannot whoop and holler, but we ride, holding on for dear life, bouncing all the way, until finally it dumps us on the shore.

I pull myself up and look at Summer. She's bent over, hands on her knees, spitting a big gooey mouthful of clear saliva on the sand. She stands up straight and slogs up onto the dry beach, dragging her boogie board behind her. Then she turns and falls into a sitting position. I sit.

I've never seen her get crushed like that before. It scares me. But she turns to me and smiles.

"I would have felt pretty bad if those were sharks and they ate you, after everything we've talked about."

I laugh. "I bet you could have punched them all in their noses. Like the Big Kahuna."

"I might have needed a little help." She shakes her head, like she can't believe all of this, the way *I* can't believe all of this. "Just so you know, I've never been that close to dolphins before."

"Really?" I ask.

"I've seen them jump plenty, but I've never been splashed by one."

"Me neither." I smile. "Obviously."

She puts her arm around me. "I'm never gonna forget that."

What she said plays in my head. I imagine myself as an old lady, sitting in a rocking chair on a porch, thinking of this, or telling it to some random young person, maybe a grandkid.

"Me neither."

Then I think of how I'll be an old lady remembering the day I got splashed by dolphins with *Summer*, and I find myself wondering whether she will be someone I still know, or just a memory like a shoebox full of seashells.

Mom isn't home for dinner. She was supposed to be home at eight, and we were gonna take a cab to a Mexican place in downtown Santa Monica. I was looking forward to telling her all about the amazing day I had today, which was almost beyond belief.

At least Summer isn't around to see me looking mopey and pathetic, eating a bowl of Raisin Bran for dinner.

I sit in the front room late into the evening, watching cartoons with the lights off. The cool night air comes through the window by the door, along with the sounds of happy people walking by on the sidewalk, strolling to and from their dinners with family and friends, going to parties. Cars drive by on Fourth Street, coming and going to restaurants and movies and the pier and everyplace else fun.

Finally the headlights of a cab make shadows on the walls of the front room as it pauses in the driveway beside the cottage. I hear Mom thank the driver, and then the shadows play in reverse as the cab backs away. Then she's putting the key in the door, turning the knob, and standing in the doorway. I feel her eyes on me.

"I didn't expect you to be up."

"I didn't expect to be *stood* up."

She watches me watching cartoons for a second, then moves to put whatever she's carrying on the big dining table. "I'm sorry, Juillet. The ER was so swamped I couldn't get away. You know how it is."

"Yep. I sure do."

I smell her Indian takeout. I hear her opening the

148

bag, taking out the containers.

"I brought aloo gobi. And vegetable korma."

It smells so good I might cry. But there's no way I'm gonna cry. "I already ate. Hours ago."

"What did you have?"

"Raisin Bran."

That sounds suitably sad in a room filled with this glorious smell. So after she gives me a chance to ask her to share, she adds, "There's enough for you if you'd like."

"No thank you."

On the screen, the guy in the cartoon who looks like he's wearing a hospital robe is flying by means of his beard.

I hear her plastic takeout utensils in the darkness. "What did you do today?" Mom asks between bites.

"Not much," I say. "Rode some sick waves on my sponge. Got splashed by some dolphins that were closer to me than you are right now."

"Really?"

"One of them was smiling at me. He jumped out of the water and grinned at me and Summer. Then he splashed us with his tail as he dove back in the water. No big deal."

"Wow! Well, if you were looking in my direction right now, you'd see that I'm smiling at you, too."

I let it hang for a moment. "I can live without that."

Saying it doesn't make me feel better. Instead it makes me feel worse, but I hope it also makes *her* feel worse. And so, without even turning in her direction, I leave Mom and her delicious-smelling aloo gobi and vegetable korma, and the cartoon guy who flies by means of his white beard, and I take my empty stomach and my empty self into my empty bedroom and shut the door harder than I should.

Standing above the nightstand, I open the drawer and look down at Mom's list, which looks back up at me.

> More exercise and fresh air.
> Confront your fears.
> Go outside your comfort zone!

Below her words are my additions.

> MAKE A NEW FRIEND
> LEARN TO SURF?
> FIX FERN THING

I start to close the drawer, but the list is noisy, hungry. I take it and flatten it on the desk, then pick up the little pencil and add words.

The newest addition is a gigantic hole in my heart, and the Fern thing is still miles away from being resolved. But looking at the first five goals—assessing my progress—I am filled with what I've done with these days of July, and I stand up straight. Through the open window I see the shapes of the moonlit blossoms shining in the sky. I take in their smells on the breeze, and allow myself to imagine that tomorrow— the Summer part of tomorrow—will be as magical as today.

15

IT'S JULY 18, and Summer and I are sitting in Adirondack chairs where the sidewalk meets the sand in front of the snack bar on the beach. The marine layer is refusing to burn off, and so the sky is as gloomy as Summer is today.

I didn't see her at all yesterday. She told me she had family stuff again. I don't know whether she goes out of her way to make me feel like I shouldn't ask for details about her family, or whether I'm just afraid for reasons entirely my own.

My phone buzzes. It's a text from Fern.

Softee's is closing forever. First you abandon me and now Softee's is closing. Hope you're having an amazing summer too!

I turn the phone screen-side down on the arm of my chair.

"Your mom?" Summer asks without cheer.

I sigh. "Fern."

A happy golden retriever comes to visit us, tail wagging. But his owner barks at him and he hurries away.

"Tell me about Lakeshore." Summer stares off toward the ocean. At least her face is pointed that way—I can't see her eyes behind the dark shades she's wearing.

I lean toward the table and take the last onion ring from the tray, then dip it into the little plastic tub of ketchup and hot sauce. "There's not much to tell."

"I remember how you described it on the first day we hung out." She digs her bare feet into the sand. "'Gross in summer, cold in winter. Jack-o'-lanterns in fall, bees in spring.'"

"Is that what I said before?"

She nods. "But I'm surprised you didn't describe it with more danger."

I take a bite of the onion ring. "What do you mean?"

She shrugs. "Something like, mosquitoes with West Nile virus in summer. Zombie hooligans on Halloween."

"Stop."

"Abominable snowman in winter. Killer bees in spring."

I take the last bite of onion ring. She's kidded me before about stupid fears, but this doesn't feel like kidding. She's not smiling.

"What happens in Lakeshore?" she asks.

"Nothing."

"What do you do?"

"Nothing. Go to the mall."

"Skating on frozen lakes?"

"Nope. Just hang out indoors under fluorescent lights."

"Shenanigans in the woods?"

"Not really." I take a sip of coconut smoothie. "I mean, there are woods and all. But I don't really go into them anymore."

She turns my way. She seems to study me for a moment while I pretend not to notice. Then she looks back to the ocean.

"There's something you're not telling me." She kicks the sand off her buried feet. "What's the worst thing that ever happened there?"

I fall back into my chair. *"Nothing."* I drop my shades from my hair to my eyes. I know she's trying to figure out why I have fears, but you don't *get* fears. You just *have* them.

"Scary video games at the arcade?"

"*Stop* it." I put my fingertips to my face and trace my features to make sure I'm scowling properly.

We don't talk for a minute. While we don't talk, people on bikes and skates and skateboards roll by on the sidewalk behind us. As we sit in silence, families play in the surf ahead in the distance. The smell of french fries and burgers and veggie tacos washes over us.

"Can I see your phone?"

I look to her. "Why?"

"Experiment." She holds her hand out, grinning like, *Please?* I lean over and pass it to her.

She taps the screen. She taps it some more. She laughs, covers her mouth.

"What?" I ask.

"I typed the letters *a* and *p* and it suggested *apocalypse*."

"No it didn't."

"Yes it did!" She puts her fingertip back to the screen. "Okay. I'm gonna put in *d* and *i*. Whoops! *Disaster!*"

"It doesn't say that."

"Yes it does!" She turns the screen to me but it's too far anyway. It's too far and I don't care. "It could have suggested any word, but it knows your personality. It knows your thinking. *Disaster* and *disease*. And *diphtheria*. Which is also some sort of disease or infection."

"I *know* what it is."

"For anyone else it might have suggested *did*. Or *didn't*. Or *dig*."

"I have no idea what your point is."

She puts my phone on the arm of my Adirondack chair. "My point is, either you're poisoning the mind of your phone, or it's poisoning yours."

I sit deep in my chair, and she falls back into hers.

A seagull lands at my feet and eats an old french fry covered in sand. Then it cocks its head, gives me a sassy look, and flies away.

"Sorry," Summer says. "I shouldn't poke fun at you."

A homeless man in dirty clothes passes us, dragging a tent toward the water. It's already assembled into its angular shape.

I take a deep breath, then let it out. "The worst thing that ever happened in Lakeshore was when my dad put his suitcases in the trunk of his car and drove to an apartment across town that he'd already rented for himself and Genevieve." I take another gulp of air. "Then the two of them moved to Switzerland, and me and my mom moved to a different part of town and a new school where I didn't know anyone because my mom was too sad to stay in the same house. There you are, since apparently you can't stand not knowing."

A lifeguard helicopter passes from north to south, a short distance out from the water's edge. The noise of the rotors wipes everything away. I close my eyes and take a deep breath. I am new.

"In Lakeshore the summer nights are the best," I say. "The sun goes down so late. Way later than dinner. Then it gets dark, and the fireflies come out." I think about when I last saw them. I can't remember if I saw them at all in June. I was probably stuck inside all month.

"I've never seen fireflies," Summer says.

"They're magical. They come on and go off. Appear and disappear. Some of the kids like to catch them and put 'em in jars. Or smear them on their skin like war paint so they can glow. But I just like to watch them appear and disappear."

"It sounds beautiful."

"I love the Little League baseball games at my school on summer nights. There's a snack bar that smells like popcorn and cotton candy. And snow cones, where you can smile and say 'Please go heavy on the syrup' when you order, at least if the boy working behind the counter has pimples and a big Adam's apple and a face that turns red when you place your order. And then when the ice is all gone and it's all melty snow-cone juice at the bottom, and the paper cone is getting soggy and almost ready to collapse, you tip it back and drink it."

"Yum," Summer says.

"And when school starts the trees are still deep green, but it's like they've been brushed with sadness. And in fall, the first cold mornings, the leaves change to bright red and yellow. And finally a dull rusty color, so you aren't so sad when they finally drop. Then the trees are completely bare and you can see everything that the woods hid all summer. Because the woods are so thick. And then they *aren't*. And then everything looks desolate until the snow falls, and it's a wonderland."

"Tell me about winter."

I listen to the distant ocean, the seagulls. A family speaking German walks by.

"When the snow falls, and it's covering everything, it's so quiet. Like every sound in the universe is absorbed by the blanket of snow. All you can hear is your own feet crunching in it. It's so quiet and bright, with white light coming from every direction."

Summer sighs. "You're lucky."

"And then in spring, when you're totally sick of cold and snow and freezing rain, the first signs of green come. It begins on things close to the ground, like hedgerows. Little bits of green. Tiny flowers.

Then *everything's* budding. People start wearing short sleeves. You hear birds singing. Once I saw a newly budding tree filled with yellow finches, like a crop of lemons. Which don't grow there. But *finches* do. In spring, when it's like the whole world comes back to life."

I imagine it. It feels like forever ago. Like another lifetime.

"Will you show me someday?"

I turn to Summer. "What part?"

"Everything. All of what you said."

I look away, to the shore, then farther, to the Santa Monica Mountains jutting into the sea to the north.

"I'd love that," I say.

"Now you remember what's nice about Lakeshore." Summer turns to me. "Like you've done for me with Ocean Park. And the waves. Letting me show you what I've loved about my life in *this* place."

I lean forward to grab an onion ring from the table, but they're all gone. So I sit back and watch the life-guard helicopter go back the other way. The light is turning a darker gray.

"The psychologists are right," I say out of nowhere. "My mom is right. My fears aren't real." I dig my feet into the sand, burying them. "I'm not afraid of zombies. Or the number three. Or tsunamis, or any of that."

Summer's hand reaches mine on the arm of my chair. I turn my palm up.

My other hand removes my shades. I wipe my eyes with the back of my arm. "Just things that ruin your life. Things that make you forget about fireflies and snow cones."

I put the shades back on my eyes. I feel pathetic.

"You didn't forget fireflies or snow cones," Summer says. "You just forgot you remembered them."

It feels good to remember the good things, and it feels good to dump the truth at Summer's feet. But I feel like there's some truth she isn't telling me, and that it's her turn to lay it down.

16

JULY 19, AND it's another day of Summer being mysteriously unavailable. I didn't ask her why she couldn't hang out when we said good-bye yesterday, but it's weird that she doesn't just tell me. I don't want to walk past her house and spy on her.

I'm also weirded out that I feel this way. That less than three weeks after meeting someone I can feel so attached and needy. It's different from the way it has been with Fern or any other friend. I used Fern to protect me from things I didn't want to do, or feel, but it feels like Summer is the key to everything I want to become.

I take a bag with my library books and grab a water at the little market on Fourth Street, then head toward the park on top of the hill. Sitting cross-legged on the cool grass in the shade of a tree that smells like a can of air freshener, I reach inside the bag and take the book my hand touches first.

Zombies Slurped My Eye Sockets at Dawn.

I look around the park. No zombies. Not even any homeless people at the moment.

I turn to the first page.

Violet was having a dream. A nice dream. She and Sully were hanging out at the convenience store like they used to, back in the old days. Back before the zombies came. They were drinking those slushy drinks with the bright colors. Violet's was red. Sully's was blue.

   "Cheers," Violet said, lifting her cup.

   "Cheers." Sully hoisted his own.

   They put their lips to the straws.

   Then, the awful slurping noise. Slurping, and screaming. Violet looked around the parking lot, but she couldn't see anyone in any kind of trouble. She looked back at Sully, who smiled and winked.

   The slurping got louder. And the screaming, rising.

   Violet bolted upright, sleep torn away. On the bunk to her right, one zombie held Sully down while another's mouth was glued to his face. Slurping.

   "My eyes!" Sully screamed. "My eyes!"

I close the book. I've seen better eye-slurping-zombie novels.

I put it back in the bag and reach for the next title.

Eat or Be Eaten.

This time I open the book to a random page near the middle.

> *For months I'd wanted Brandonne to give me exactly the hungry look he was giving me now. But I never dreamed he'd give me this look with a spear in one hand and ketchup packets in the other. Or that I'd be gazing back at him, salivating, holding a small hatchet and a squeeze bottle of horseradish sauce. But we were the last Morsels, and this was what our lives had come to.*
>
> *My stomach growled—roared! I flipped the top of the horseradish bottle, and gripped the hatchet tightly. Then I slowly advanced upon the boy I once loved.*

I sigh, and shut the book. Then I drop it in the bag and lie back on the grass.

The breeze asks me to close my eyes. The birds sing me a song. It seems like a good day for a daydream, if I can remember how.

But with my eyes closed, I can't daydream. Instead I find myself wondering why Summer has been acting more mysterious every day, and sadder. It's like while she's been rubbing off on me, I've been rubbing off on her. Then I wonder if maybe there's been something dark underneath her sunny exterior all along.

17

THE NEXT AFTERNOON, we ignore alien orders at two. I arrive first and wait for Summer. I watch as she walks up the sidewalk, her face pointed down. She looks like she's frowning, until she raises her eyes and sees me. She puts on a smile, the first smile that's ever felt unconvincing on her. As she gets closer, she gives me a weird look.

"What?"

"Hello," she says.

"Hello back. Why are you looking at me that way?"

"Because." She reaches to me and pokes my shoulder. "I was thinking about how you were made up on the day we first met."

"Oh."

"And even more on the second day. Like a punk-rock corpse doll."

I'm not sure what to think of this, so I shift from one foot to the other.

"It was a fun look," she says, like she's just decided.

"Fun?"

"Kind of Halloweeny."

I maybe frown a little.

"But *so* cute."

I look down at my bare feet. "Thanks."

"Did you run out of makeup?"

"No. I guess I just haven't been using it lately."

She gasps. "You know what would be fun?"

"What?"

"You be me and I'll be you!"

"What do you mean?"

"Make me up like a corpse doll! And you can be whatever I am. Just for today."

I'm suddenly not so excited. "I don't think I can be *you*." By which I mean a gorgeous surfer girl.

Summer pushes me away with both hands, but playfully. "You totally can! Come on, let's get your makeup!"

I follow her to the cottage Mom and I are staying in. She walks around the hedge and to the door, like it's *her* cottage, like she's been friends with every kid who's ever stayed here. I wonder if she *has* been.

Summer waits for me to open the door, then follows me back to the bathroom. I open the medicine cabinet, then look at her.

"You sure about this?"

She nods fervently. "I wanna look just like *you* did when I first saw you at Pinkie Promise."

I sigh. "Okay. It'll be ruining a good thing, but okay."

I take her and my makeup bag into my bedroom and sit her on the bed, where the light from the window reveals the perfection of her glowing skin.

Perched on a stool in front of her, I begin with pale foundation, which in Summer's case needs several applications to cover her glow. Then ivory powder, black eye shadow, black eyeliner above and below, and three passes of mascara. Just like me, back on the second day of July. Summer gradually disappears behind the makeup until she's someone else entirely, someone I don't recognize. Then I put her long golden hair into several ponies, doubled over to shorten them. They stick out of her head like demon horns.

I lean back to take in the sight of her, grinning back at me, and the drama of her appearance makes my heart hammer. She looks like the beautiful warrior princess of the walking dead.

"How do I look?"

"Amazing."

She jumps up and runs to the bathroom. She screams with happiness.

"I *love* it!"

I stand and join her in the bathroom, and look over her shoulder at her reflection.

"I'm sad," she says to her mirrored self.

"It's just makeup."

"My life is a tragedy."

"It comes off with makeup remover."

"Zombies are coming to slurp my eye sockets dry!" She puts on an expression of grief, then looks at me in the reflection with a smile that doesn't seem real, and doesn't seem hers. "Now you!"

I look at my face, which looks terribly uninteresting by comparison. "I can't be you."

"Of course you can! You've already got darker skin than the day you arrived. Kinda like you're blushing. And we can mess up your hair and then spray it with hairspray so it looks like it's stiff with salt water. Then you can wear a bathing suit and I can wear your clothes." Her eyes get big. "I wanna wear your *DEATH* T-shirt!"

We mess up my hair with four hands, then use hairspray found in the cupboard to get it all stiff like a day in the ocean does. She dresses as me in my black *DEATH* tee, ripped jeans, and black Converse high-tops with the skulls and crossbones painted on the sides. Of course Summer looks much better as me than *I* ever did.

I dress as her, but in my own two-piece swimsuit. After a couple of weeks in the sun, my feet no longer look like they belong to a dead person. After all the swimming and boogie boarding, my limbs look almost like they belong to an athlete. But I'm no Summer.

"Let's go out and show the world!" Summer says.

Out the door, around the hedge, down the hill we go. She stops short when we get to Third Street.

"I can't cross this street!" she says dramatically.

I frown. "Are you making fun of me?"

She shakes her head. "Please walk me across while I close my eyes!"

I do.

We continue down the hill, then cross Main Street. Everyone we pass stares at Summer, because she's a stunning punk-rock corpse doll. They stare at her like maybe they recognize her, but can't remember where from.

Two more blocks and we're crossing the park, then into the sand.

"I'm afraid of the seagulls!" she shouts. "And the

water, and tsunamis and salt and seaweed and mermaids!" She looks at me expectantly, like I'm supposed to respond.

"It'll be okay," I say dejectedly. "You can hold my hand."

We walk to the water, hands joined. Instead of stopping at the edge, she keeps walking into the noisy surf. She pulls me until she's wearing my jeans and shoes in waist-deep water.

"This is weird," I say. "This isn't fun."

She pushes on, heading deeper. I fight to hold her back.

"Why are you doing this?" I try to dig in my heels, but she's stronger than me.

"My turn, Juillet! My turn to be sad!"

"Summer! You're scaring me!"

"Don't call me Summer! I'm tired of being Summer!"

She's wild-eyed, crazed. Dark clouds sweep in from the ocean, stranger in July than a bluebird wave. Summer looks like a witch from the depths, conjuring them.

I drop her hand and take a step away from her. "Please stop it!"

The black ocean roils. Whitecaps burst from sharp-peaked waves.

"It won't stop!" she shouts.

I'm genuinely terrified of her. She's like a girl from one of the books I've been reading, suddenly demonic from the bite of a zombie.

Then she breaks down crying. Her face shows agony, she doubles over, her hair dipping into the ocean. Her body is wracked with sobs as the waves crash against her.

Finally she unbends, and slogs through the water, away from the deep, until she hits the beach. She drops to the sand on her knees, her back to the sea.

I get on my knees beside Summer. I listen while her sobs calm and her breathing quiets, until the only sound is the ocean's roar.

I put my hand on her back. "What's wrong?" I feel clumsy trying to console her.

Summer finally raises her head, wipes snot away from her nose. The black makeup is smeared from the surf, like the biggest cry ever.

"I have to show you something." She rises to her feet, and begins trudging across the dry sand, face-down.

I follow alongside as we cross the beach, my mind racing, wondering what she's going to show me. A million questions race through my head, but I can't voice them. And Summer is silent as we leave the sand, walking the first blocks and across Main Street. The

only sound is the squish of her wet shoes and jeans—
my wet shoes and jeans—that she's wearing.

Up Hill Street we go, and down Fourth. Walking
the sidewalk, to the house with the driveway leading
to the two-story garage behind. Instead of going past,
we turn down the driveway made of pavers with grass
growing between them in a geometric pattern. They
feel good underfoot.

The garage isn't a garage anymore—it's two stories of house the color of the sky. Summer opens the
door and leads me inside, revealing the world she's
been hiding from me.

Inside, the decor is cheery. I quickly note that there
is an elevator, but I follow her up the stairs, holding
the white-painted rail, to the second floor. Summer
pauses on the landing and turns to me. She speaks
quietly.

"These are the rules. No sadness. No crying. Expect
the best outcomes. Don't feel sorry. Be positive. Okay?"

"Okay."

I heard the rules, but I have no idea what is about to
happen. I feel my chest tightening as Summer knocks
on the door to the right and peeks her head inside,
speaking to someone within.

"Can I have a second with my brother?"

I don't hear a response, but in a moment a

middle-aged woman in a nurse's uniform leaves the room. She looks Summer up and down, at her wet clothes and smeary Goth makeup, then eyes me critically as she passes.

Summer motions for me to follow her inside. "Hey, Shreddy Freddy!" she says, her tone suddenly cheerful. She moves her sunglasses from her eyes to her hair. "I want you to meet a friend. Betty, this is my big brother, Hank. Hank, this is my new friend, Betty."

"Actually it's Juillet," I say. I say it even though it seems incredibly unimportant as I stand rooted to the wood floor in the doorway, staring at a withered young man in what looks like a hospital bed.

"Looks like Maria is giving you the silent treatment again." Summer turns on a bedside radio to the classical station as Hank stares blankly across the room. "Come in," she says to me. "He won't bite. I *wish* he would bite, but he won't. He gets all his meals through a feeding tube. Twice a day. Yumzers."

She sits in a chair at his side and directs me into another. I step over the power cords that connect to the bed, and move in beside Summer.

"Hank is my favorite person in the whole world," she says, moving his hair off his forehead. Hank doesn't seem to notice. "He's the best junior surfer in SoCal. And he's itching to get back out there to shred."

Summer wipes her nose with the back of her arm. "We used to have some epic times together." She leans in to pat him on the shoulder. "We still do."

She seems to be speaking for his benefit and not mine, but his expression doesn't change. He looks the way Summer would look if Summer were a boy who never ate, never saw the sun, never got out of bed.

"The doctors say he's in a vegetative state, but I've been studying up on it, and I think it's more like what's called a *minimally conscious state*. Which has a much better prognosis. He doesn't even need a respirator, 'cause he's got such strong lungs. And when I read him something funny, sometimes out of the corner of my eye I see him smile. And he still likes stories and music, and being wheeled onto the balcony to watch the ocean. You can see it over the trees and rooftops. I would suggest we do that right now, but it looks like Maria of the Constant Sorrows is in the middle of giving him a sponge bath. Which means he's already had his massage. Am I right?"

She's asking Hank, but he stares across the room, oblivious. I try not to stare at him. Instead my eyes take in the bowl and the sponges, the comb, the copy of *The Old Man and the Sea* beside the lamp on the table. The room is awash in an antiseptic smell. French doors open to a balcony with a view of the ocean, several impossibly distant blocks away.

"Anyway, Betty and I are gonna go have some kicks. I'll be back to read to you later. Okay? Don't let Maria turn off the music. I love you."

She bends over him and kisses his cheek. He doesn't notice.

"Betty loves you too," she says. "She's been dying to meet you."

She's telling him all kinds of lies that can't make him feel better, 'cause I'm pretty sure he can't hear them.

"Bye, Hank," I say. "It was nice to meet you."

I smile, for Hank or myself or Summer, and I follow her out of the room. She shuts the door behind us, then takes a deep breath, pauses, and lets it out. Then she nods. "Come on."

I follow her down the stairs.

In the living room, Maria the caregiver rises from an easy chair as Summer points to the ceiling and leads me out the front door.

We walk in silence down the sidewalk toward Ocean Park Boulevard. I want to say things that will make her feel better, but I don't know what those things are, or if they even exist. I want to ask questions, but I don't know *which* questions, and I'm afraid that whatever she says to answer will only end with her feeling worse.

We walk down Ocean Park past Third Street, which seems just embarrassing now, that I was ever afraid to cross it. Then down to Main, over to Hollister, up to Second, across to Hill, and finally I notice we aren't going anywhere. I'm afraid that she's walking to lose me, that she wants me to disappear but she's too nice to say it.

Finally she stops and turns to me. "Can we write postcards?"

"Sure."

She walks quickly down to Main Street, like she's angry, and I follow alongside. She dips inside a used-bookstore with a musty smell, and grabs a stack of postcards from a kiosk. There are about twenty, all of them with the same image of an ancient old lady in a bikini, who looks very much like Gladys from the Beachcombers garbage patrol.

"These," she says, slapping them on the counter.

"Hey, Summer." The old hippie behind the counter smiles at her. "That's an interesting look you're sporting today." He raises his eyebrows at me, questioning. I shrug at him.

Summer pays, gets her change. Then we go next

door to a vegan place and she drops into a chair at one of the tables on the sidewalk. I sit across from her.

"Pen!" She looks around, annoyed. "I need a pen!"

I get up and go inside. The place is empty, but the food smells good. Behind the counter is a girl with dreadlocks and a nose ring. She gives me a pen. I return to Summer, present it to her. She accepts it without thanks and begins scribbling hurriedly on one of the postcards. I look away, at the display window of the adjoining bookstore. It features old vinyl records from Bob Dylan and Jimi Hendrix, and tattered copies of books by Sylvia Plath and Jack Kerouac. I've never read them. Maybe I will one day.

"Here." Summer holds a postcard to me. I take it from her, and she begins scribbling on the next postcard.

I look at the writing on the one she's given me. It's manic, messy.

Thank you for the pen. Sorry I am not happy at this moment.

I think about saying *you're welcome*, and *it's okay, you don't always have to be happy*, but I don't. She hands me another postcard, and when I take it, she continues writing on the next.

Hank got hurt the night of his eighth-grade graduation. He and some friends were horsing around on the promenade. On a fountain. Posing for a picture behind a sign that says stay off the fountain. He slipped and fell hard on his head, then practically drowned in knee-deep water.

I look up from the postcard, then take a breath. I watch Summer write, and I'm ready for it when she hands me the next one.

The best junior surfer in SoCal nearly drowned in a fountain. It wasn't even something momentous, like the biggest wave ever. It was something stupid that wasn't even very fun.

I feel tears welling up, but Summer looks angry. She hands me another postcard.

For the first day he seemed like he would be okay. He was in the hospital but he could talk. Then his

*brain swelled uncontrollably and he
got worse and worse.*

I imagine it, what she writes. I feel it all.

*For a long time I couldn't go to the
promenade or pass by the fountain.*

She has slowed down. She searches for words now, instead of spilling them. She slides one more postcard across the table to me.

*We've had a rule that there's no
sadness allowed in Hank's room. So all
I can do is watch him waste away and
pretend everything is going to be
okay.*

I look up from the postcard. She's looking at me.

"Hank was supposed to be the Big Kahuna," Summer says.

"What do you mean?"

Her eyes lower to the table in front of her. "The Big Kahuna is always the most important surfer on the beach. Every good beach has one. It has to be a surfer who makes it look easy, whose board is an extension of their body. And they need to be able to settle every argument just by showing up. Nobody cuts in the lineup when the Big Kahuna is on the water. And everyone knew that when the Big Kahuna faded into the sunset, it would be Hank's turn." She shakes her head. "This is bad for Ocean Park. This is bad for everyone."

I watch her stillness, her faraway eyes. I feel like she's wishing for me to have a solution, or a different reality for her. Or maybe it's me wishing I did.

"Wait." She gets up from the table and goes inside. She speaks to the girl with the dreadlocks and the nose ring, who gives her a key attached to a plastic beach bucket. Summer uses it to open the bathroom door, and goes inside.

I leave the postcards on the table and hurry into the café.

Through the bathroom door I hear Summer crying. *Loudly*. She tells the universe how much she hates it. She also hates the promenade and the fountain.

The girl with the dreadlocks and the nose ring appears in front of me, then puts her hands together in the namaste pose and does a little bow. "Um, do you think she's likely to harm any of our inanimate friends in there?"

"Do you mean break stuff?"

The girl nods, bows again.

"I'm not sure." I look from the girl to the bathroom door. "I don't think so. I've never seen her like this before."

Through the door the wailing continues. It's breaking my heart.

"Perhaps a delicious, fresh, organic juice would make her feel better?"

"Maybe. Sure."

The girl hurries behind the counter, where I am dimly aware of her movements, busy with the juicing apparatus.

Summer keeps crying and wailing, at times incoherently. But as the volume of her grief diminishes, and the volume of the juicer rises, I hear her say the most heartbreaking thing.

Sea, swallow me.

"Summer?" There's no response. There's no more wailing. "Please come out."

I wait.

Then, finally, "It sucks out there."

I look around. The vegan café is charming enough, but she's right.

"Yes it does," I say. "But it'd be much better with you by my side." I wait, listening. "I need you."

After a moment the door lock clicks, the knob turns. Summer comes out, tear-streaked and disheveled.

"You look like you need a hug," she says.

"So do you."

I hold her against me. She holds me against her.

Then the girl with the dreadlocks and the nose ring appears, holding a glass of delicious-looking juice.

"Um, I hate to ask, but did you leave the bucket with the key inside the bathroom?"

Summer drinks the juice from a straw as we sit at the table outside. She noisily slurps the remains sticking to the glass, then sighs a sigh of resolve. "I have just one more favor to ask."

"You can ask as many favors as you need to."

"I need to talk to Hank. I need to break all the rules of his room. And I need you to be with me for courage."

"Okay." She's asking the wrong girl, I think. But I'll do my best.

We walk back up the hill to Fourth Street, then back up the stairs, back to Hank's room. The sun is lower, flooding the room with the light of late afternoon. Summer stands for a while in the doorway, watching him. Then she sits again in the chair closest to Hank's bed, and I sit beside her.

"You never made me feel like a nuisance, like an uncool little sister. All my life, you always made me feel like a princess."

She reaches to Hank and fidgets with the collar of his pajamas.

"You were so patient, teaching me to surf. Every day after school. Even dawn patrol on schooldays. And when I finally caught my first wave and rode it in, with you beside me, you looked so excited. Like it was *your* first wave."

She strokes his cheek with the back of her hand.

"Then you and Otis carried me over your heads on my board like I was royalty, going down the beach, bragging to everyone we passed, talking like it was the sickest wave ever, the sickest *ride* ever." She shakes her head, slowly. "I don't think I'll ever feel as happy as I did in that moment. Blowing kisses at everyone we passed like I was showering them with the magic I felt. And you were so proud of me." She chokes back a sob. "I want you to always be proud of me. Like I am of you."

I reach to Summer, put my hand on her shoulder. I want to say *of course he'll be proud of you*, but instead I say nothing.

"I know you're leaving," she whispers in his ear, her voice catching. "And I'm gonna miss you so, so much."

Her face is almost unrecognizable in its sadness.

Then she crawls onto the bed beside him. Her head rests against Hank's, her arm draped across his shallow chest. With her smeary Goth makeup, she looks like the dead visiting the dying.

I watch Summer lie at Hank's side. I watch my hands, folded between my knees. I decide that when I get back to the cottage, I'm going to add another goal to the list.

HELP SUMMER LIKE SHE HAS HELPED ME

I gaze beyond the balcony at the distant lines of breakers moving in to the shore. When I look back at Summer, she's asleep.

18

THE NEXT DAY, Summer's sadness seems almost forgotten. Like every day she begins brand-new, a sun
born that very morning. At least that's what it looks
like.

She and I are down on Main Street, and Summer
is riding Hank's skateboard while I carry hers. I've
only been on a skateboard for about five minutes in
my whole life, and this sidewalk has too many bumps
and people and dogs and benches for me to trust my
limited ability. Summer, meanwhile, is riding like she
was born with a skateboard attached to her feet.

Farther down the sidewalk I see the two mean boys.
Wade and his sidekick. They're on their skateboards
too, heading our direction.

Then Summer sees them. She stops suddenly in

front of a secondhand store called Driftwood, and kicks her board up into her hands.

"Let's check this place out! They always have cool stuff."

I follow her inside. It's one of the many narrow stores lined up shoulder to shoulder on Main Street, and it's stuffed full of strange things. Lots of vintage clothes, but objects, too. As we enter, a woman looks up from behind the counter and smiles, but otherwise we have the place to ourselves.

We poke around the clothing racks. "Check it! Vintage." Summer calls from across the store. She's holding up an older version of the Beachcombers T-shirt. "I can wear this and look like I've been scouring the beach for garbage since before I was born. Dude, this might have belonged to Gladys when she was our age!"

I smile. My fingers trail over a low shelf of books. Then I bump into a bench, which sits before a piano.

I lay Summer's skateboard on the bench and sit beside it, then put my fingers to the keys. It's been so long since my fingers have been here.

In my head I hear a song I learned a few years ago. I've been hearing it on the Beach Boys channel Mom has been playing constantly at the cottage. "Wouldn't It Be Nice." It's a cheerful song, even though it's entirely about things not being the way they should be, and whenever I hear it playing, it's somehow easier to think about all the things in life I wish were different. Like maybe it isn't hopeless to dream. Or maybe dreaming is the only possible sweetness when everything in the world isn't what it should be.

I close my eyes. My hands find their way to the keys. I visit notes with my fingers, hear them with my ears. It's been a while since I've sat at a piano, so we spend a few seconds getting reacquainted.

Then I nod *one, two, three, four,* and begin playing.

It's been years since I've played the song, but my hands know how to bring the sounds from the keyboard.

My eyes stay closed, and I listen to myself play. The piano isn't terribly out of tune. The acoustics in the shop aren't bad, with the echo of the cement floor muted by the racks of clothing. And my playing isn't too shabby, though maybe my tempo is a bit slow. Like I'm having a hard time feeling the sunniness written into it.

I play through just the first stanza, hearing the lyrics, to the part about the world where we belong. Then I open my eyes and see Summer standing beside the bench.

"Don't stop!"

"Were you singing?"

"No. *Yes*. A little."

My hands withdraw from the keyboard. "Your voice sounded pretty."

"Your playing sounded *amazing*! You didn't tell me you could do that."

I think about saying *thank you*, and I think about saying *you didn't ask*. But instead, and out of nowhere, I dump a truth that has been haunting me for weeks.

"Piano is kinda my thing. It always has been. The reason my mom made me stop hanging out with Fern is because I missed a big piano recital. I told my mom that Fern had a premonition of something terrible happening at my recital, and that I was afraid to go. I was hiding out at the mall while my mom was trying to find me."

Summer looks at me, waiting for more.

"It was easy for my mom to believe it, because Fern is shy and superstitious. And because she likes to hang out at the mall and think about the end of the world. She loves having séances for dead pets, and talking to spirits with a Ouija board. So she's kinda dark and creepy. But she *didn't* tell me something terrible would happen at my recital."

My hands return to the keys.

"Fern isn't famous for having a lot of friends because

she's so . . . odd. But she makes me laugh. And she's kind." I turn back to the keys. "She deserves to have a friend. But I don't deserve her."

I strike the first notes of the Haydn composition I was supposed to play months ago at my recital, then pause, and again find my way into the opening of "Wouldn't It Be Nice." I halt after the intro.

"Thank you for telling me all of that." I feel Summer's hand on my left shoulder. "But what's the real reason you didn't go to the recital? Did Ms. Sardinia tell you something bad would happen at the recital?"

I don't answer, because I'm not ready, not just yet. But as I stare over the piano, I think about the man who ruined my life. The man who used to read to me at bedtime, who taught me how to play catch, who loved listening to me play the piano, who always sat in the front row at my recitals, who—

My thoughts are interrupted by the sound of my own hands banging the keys, once, in anger. The mixed notes hang in the air like bad feelings.

"Sorry," I call out to the shopkeeper.

If I had blamed Mistress Scarfia, maybe I could still hang out with Fern.

If I had told the truth, I could definitely still hang out with Fern.

Even though I didn't answer Summer's simple

question, Summer—instead of leaving, instead of walking away from the girl who betrayed Fern—sits beside me on the bench.

"Play it. Play 'Wouldn't It Be Nice.'" She leans into me for emphasis. "Play it and I'll sing. I know all the words. And it's exactly the song we both need right now."

So I play. And Summer sings. And though the keys are blurry through my teary eyes, and though Summer's voice gets choked up at a couple of points, it is—as Summer said—exactly the song we both need.

A short while later we're on the boardwalk. I'm fastening the strap of my helmet, watching skaters and people on bikes and scooters and every kind of wheeled transport rolling by. It really isn't a boardwalk, but rather a sidewalk that goes for miles along the beach from Venice to Pacific Palisades.

"Isn't there, like, a giant empty parking lot we can do this in?"

"Not in Dogtown," Summer answers. "Anyway, this is perfect. No hills. No cars."

I look down at my ride. It's Summer's skateboard. She's gonna ride Hank's. Summer said she learned to ride a skateboard before she learned to surf, and she thinks they're enough alike that it'll be good to do it this way.

"Which foot do I put in front again?"

"Left foot. Unless it feels really weird, in which case you're goofy-footed, and you can switch to the right foot. But only if it makes you feel mental to have the left foot in front."

I'm pretty sure that I'll be goofy-footed, 'cause it just sounds like me. But I put my left foot, wearing my black Converse, down on the front end of the skateboard. Immediately I fall on my butt, and the board rolls away, veering off the two-lane sidewalk and onto the sand.

"You did that great," Summer says, giving me a hand and pulling me up. "But try not to fall on your butt. Keep your weight over the board. You fell off there because you were kinda behind it."

I fetch the board and get on again, left foot in front, balanced over the deck, remembering what she said. I push off with my right foot and roll slowly forward.

"Steer by leaning just a bit to one side or the other," she says. "This sidewalk is nice and straight with very slow curves."

I give a kick with my right foot, then another. Then my right joins my left, behind it on the deck.

"Very good," she says. She's directly behind me. We're going so slow because *I'm* going so slow. People on skates and skateboards and bikes move around us to pass.

"See if you can go a little faster," Summer says. "And when we hit this curve up here, you can practically steer just by tilting your head."

"Got it." I kick twice and roll faster. Summer keeps up behind me effortlessly. I kick once, twice, three times, and I'm rolling along smoothly.

"Don't slow down for the bend," she says. So I kick three more times. I bend back at the waist just a bit, tilting my head to the left, and the board beneath me does the same. I take the curve perfectly, then straighten up as the sidewalk does.

"Beautiful!" she shouts. "You're a natural!" Then she kicks until she's at my side, grinning. "Hey, Betty!"

I look at her and immediately swerve to the right. The wheels catch in the sand and I fall into it. Summer stops expertly, then falls intentionally in the sand beside me.

"It's not about how many times you fall down," she says. "It's about getting back up over and over until you begin to feel like you were born with wheels for feet."

I stand. She stands beside me.

"I have wheels for feet," I say.

Summer looks down at them, squinting. "I think you're right. I can see them sprouting."

I put the board back on the sidewalk and step my feet onto it. I kick, kick, kick, tilt left briefly to center myself in the lane. People pass us less frequently, then not at all. The people coming the other direction down the sidewalk no longer look at me like I'm a hazard.

By the time we get to the pier, Summer can ride at my side without me freaking out and falling down. We ride all the way to Pacific Palisades and back, and by then I truly do have wheels for feet.

Later we're sitting at a table on the sidewalk at Smoothie Tsunami, a cute place on Main Street with fresh flowers in glass jars on all the tables. I would have probably been afraid to hang out at a place with *tsunami* in its name three weeks ago. But here I am.

"Here we go." Summer takes an assortment of postcards from her little mesh purse, which she's carrying instead of her big beach bag. Summer says we're writing therapy postcards. I don't know exactly what she means by that, but I'm about to find out. "Okay, I'll start. I write the first line and then you write the next, then me, and so forth."

"Okay."

She leans back in her chair and bites the pen she holds.

I watch a guy roll by on his skateboard with his hands held together in the namaste position. This town is filled with people doing the namaste thing with their hands.

Summer leans forward and writes on the postcard, then turns it over and slides it across the table to me.

"Special delivery." She scoots the pen my way.

The postcard shows a dolphin wearing sunglasses, with white sunscreen on its nose. I turn it over.

Dear Fern,

I look to Summer. "Why?"

She shrugs. "I don't know. We'll find out. That's the point."

I look back at the card with all its empty space. I pick up the pen, and put the tip to the card.

I am spending July in a place called Ocean Park.

I turn it over and send it back to Summer, along with the pen. She looks at it, smiles. She writes quickly and slides it back.

There are no malls.

Now *I* smile. I put my words down.

Instead there are sidewalks to skateboard on.

I push it back to Summer. She responds quickly.

And waves to ride.

I think hard about how to word my next line.

And a girl named Summer who makes me feel brave instead of afraid. Who makes me feel like a butterfly instead of a caterpillar stuck in her cocoon.

I slide it back to Summer. She stares at the words, then puts her hand on her heart. She takes a deep breath, holds it, and lets it out. Her eyes return to mine.

"I think this one is done." She slides it back to me, along with a blank postcard. "Now you start."

"Wait," I say. "I need to write a little more to Fern."

Summer gives me a curious look, and one corner of her mouth turns up. "Okay. Feel it."

There's no more room on the first postcard, so I start fresh on the next one, which shows a surfer-girl emoji on the front. I begin writing in tiny letters, because I've got a feeling it'll take quite a few words to say what I need to say.

Dear Fern—

I'm so sorry. I lied to my mom, telling her that you made me afraid to go to my piano recital, that you had a premonition that something bad would happen there. The truth is I was afraid of feeling heartbroken that my dad wouldn't be there, sitting in the front row, that I'd be too sad to play, thinking of him being far away with some woman who isn't my mom. But my mom is right in saying I shouldn't spend so much time at the mall. I want to have adventures, and I want to have adventures with you. Can we do that? Talk to you in August? Please forgive me.

Juillet

I turn it over, print-side down. "Sorry I didn't leave you any room. I think I need to put a stamp on this one."

I slide it to Summer, who reads it, then shakes her head.

"I wish I could say the things I need to say like you do. Definitely put a stamp on this one."

There's someone else I need to write to, so I take a fresh postcard from the short stack. This one shows an old lady buried in sand up to her head. Sand dollars cover her eyes. I half smile and turn it over. Then I feel my face get serious, and I write one word.

Dad—

I pause, then put it print-side down and slide it to Summer. She turns it over, looks at me like I've punched her in the stomach.

She looks down again, and her hair falls across her eyes, but she doesn't brush it away. She writes briefly, slides it back.

I'm so mad at you for leaving.

She's right. I elaborate.

You ruined life for me and Mom.

Back to Summer. She looks at me, writes, returns it.

*And even if Hank can't see or hear, I
know it hurts him too.*

My jaw drops. I look at Summer. "Whose dad are
we talking about?"

She raises her eyebrows, points to herself, pokes her
own rib cage.

"He *left*?"

She nods.

"After Hank got hurt?"

She nods again. "He's a cinematographer for a cable
series being shot in Hungary. There's a million jobs
like that in LA, but he's acting like the only one for
him is in a place halfway across the world where he
doesn't have to see Hank wither away. He's only here
like two days every month."

I reach across the table to her. She puts her hand
in mine, but tips her chin down and shakes her long
golden hair into her face.

We stay this way for some time. I look at the deeply
tanned skin of the hand holding mine, the tiny blond
hairs on her arm. I watch people walk past on the
sidewalk, as they look at us and wonder what they are
seeing. And *I* am wondering what they are seeing.

Finally she tilts her head up and shakes her hair out
of her face. She's trying to look invincible.

"*You* wouldn't have left," she says.

I shake my head.

"I didn't know you when all that happened," she says, "but if I did know you, you wouldn't have left."

I shake my head again. I hope I wouldn't have left.

"Because you're the strongest, bravest person I know," she says.

I smile at the strangeness of what she says. Part of me is starting to believe that she may be right, and part of me thinks that maybe I would have stayed not because I'm brave but because I'm the opposite of brave.

19

AFTER A MORNING spent riding the sidewalks, we ditch our skateboards at our homes up on the hill. It's really starting to *feel* like home after three weeks, like I actually live here, and more and more of me wishes I did. I tell this to Summer as we again ignore alien orders. I've changed into my shorty, and so has Summer. She's got a pink surfboard under one arm, sea-foam green under the other.

"You're almost ready." She grins. "You've got gills. Your hands are becoming fins."

I look at them, left and right. The black polish on my fingernails has nearly worn away, but there's more to my transformation than that. It's also how I *feel*. This hill has gotten smaller. The dark green sea, shining in the distance, is the fragrance of my skin and hair.

"But first we need to get you comfortable on a stick. You can use my board." Summer turns so the pink one is facing me. "And I'll use Hank's."

I take the pink board from her. She says it's made of fiberglass, and it's considerably heavier than the boogie boards we've been riding the last couple of weeks. Standing, it's a little taller than I am. I arrange it under my arm and we begin walking down the sidewalk.

"A lot of surf schools use longer boards, like nine feet," Summer says. "And that length is easier to stand on. But they're brutal when you're trying to go out in the break zone again and again, plowing through the rakers." She makes the turn onto Ocean Park Boulevard, and I follow. "It's like wrestling a crocodile."

"Can we not talk about crocodiles?"

"These short boards are a bit trickier to stay on, but they're more fun, and they're light, so you get lots more chances to stay on a wave before you get exhausted. If we were carrying nine-foot boards, you'd be done by the time we got to the water. Anyway, today we'll just practice on the sand. And take pictures." She indicates the little mesh bag on her shoulder.

Down the hill we go. We pass beneath the hummingbird buffet in the high blossoms atop the Dr.

Seuss stalks. As we cross Third Street, being afraid of the number three seems like a distant memory. Like a bad dream I've woken from.

My arms and legs are stronger than when Mom and I arrived in Ocean Park, from all this walking and carrying and skating and swimming. So the beach seems nearer than it once did, and the surfboard being heavier than the boogie board ends up not being a big deal. I only change arms three times before we arrive at the water's edge.

"This must be the place," Summer says. She lays her board on the sand, just before where it gets damp, pointing it at the sea. "Lay your board next to mine."

I do.

She gestures at the ocean. "Obviously when we're surfing we'll be facing the shore instead of the sea, but looking at the water is nicer."

"Right."

"But first we have to pray to the surf gods." She drops and sits cross-legged on her board, doing a sort of lotus pose with her eyes closed. I stand watching until she opens her eyes and frowns at me. "Come on! You mustn't anger them."

I look around us and see that practically everyone is watching Summer, but for the usual reasons. She seems to be pulling it off, this weird behavior, so I lower myself to the pink board and sit cross-legged.

"Opposable thumbs!" Summer barks.

I comply, making loops of my index fingers and thumbs, the backs of my hands resting on my knees. Like I'm meditating in some temple with incense and gongs.

Summer glances at me and smiles. "Repeat after me. *Oh, gods of the waves.*"

"Do we have to do this?"

"Only if you want to catch a wave."

I'm still frowning.

"And this worked pretty well when Hank taught *me* to surf."

It's impossible to refuse when she puts it *that* way. I sit up straight.

"Repeat. *Oh, gods of the waves.*"

"Oh, gods of the waves."

"*Neptune, Little Mermaid, Charlie Tuna, legions of sea monkeys.*"

"Neptune, Little Mermaid, Charlie Tuna, and sea monkeys."

"*Please allow me to bum a ride on the sick crest of your fury.*"

"Please allow me to bum a ride on the sick crest of your fury."

"*And do no harm to my cute friend Juillet.*" In the

corner of my eye I see her smiling.

"And do no harm to my friend Summer."

"Boom shaka-laka."

"Boom shaka-laka."

She jumps to her feet, and I stand. She shows me how to attach the leash of the surfboard to my back ankle. Then she begins instructing me on how to position myself on the board before the wave comes, either on my knees or lying down on my belly. How to cup my hands to paddle fastest when the wave comes. She gets back to her feet, and so do I.

"The surf schools teach people to pop up with this one, two, three, four thing. But by the time you go through all the positions and get to four you're either crushed or the wave has left you behind. You really need to just throw yourself from position one to position four."

"Will I be able to do that?"

Summer swings her arm toward me, taps my shoulder. "Of course! Probably. Those yoga poses have built up your strength. And all the boogie boarding. Okay, watch me."

She lies back down, belly to her board. She looks over her shoulder.

"Okay, here comes the wave. I scoop the water to get some speed. Left, right, left, right. When it kisses my toes, just before it stands me on my nose, I throw myself from position one to position four."

Like a spring she flies to a crouched position, feet parallel. She rises slowly, unbending until she is half-standing.

"Both my feet are straddling the spine of the board. Front foot right in the middle. Back one about a foot's length from the end of the tail."

She shows me how the surf pose is similar to the warrior pose, but with both hands pointing forward, my right arm across my body. She calls it the surf warrior. She says that putting more weight on my front foot makes me go faster, and more pressure on my back foot slows me down. She says that steering is pretty much like a skateboard. She tells me that after I ride the wave in, I should bail in the shallow water rather than come up on the sand, which is fine with a boogie board but apparently not with surfing.

"You're gonna wipe out every now and then," she says. It's the first thing she's said that I'm sure I can do. "And when you do, you wanna try to go back-ward, and throw your arms and legs out to slow you down." She takes a step toward me, and speaks with an uncharacteristic seriousness. "If by any chance you fall forward, especially headfirst, cover your face and head with your arms. Like this." She puts her hands on the back of her head, her elbows pointing at me. "Show me."

I do what she did. Like my arms are a bicycle helmet.

Summer nods. "Good. Now let's practice the pop-up."

It's my turn to get on my belly, palms facedown on the board beneath my ribs.

"Okay, your position is good. Look over your shoulder."

I look over my shoulder. I see the snack bar, but I pretend I see a wave rising.

"Scoop some water. This one looks primo."

I scoop at the sand, picking up speed on an imaginary swell.

"Palms to the deck!"

I bring my hands beneath my ribs on the board, my palms flat but flexed, ready to spring.

"Jump!"

I throw myself to my feet, twisting to my right. Miraculously I land in a crouch, and though I almost lose my balance and fall back on the sand, I stay on my feet. I rise to the surf warrior and move my arms to the left, toward the nose of the board.

"Betty! That was amazing!" Summer walks in a circle around me, observing my form. "But don't stand too quickly," she says. "Unbend your knees slowly so you can make sure you're properly balanced. You don't want to be anywhere close to vertical until after the drop."

"The drop?"

"Yeah, that's when you ride down the face of the wave. It happens really fast, but it's the best part. If you can stay on the board through the drop, you've got a good chance of having a killer ride."

I keep listening to everything she says as I practice lying facedown on the board, paddling scoops of sand that we're pretending are water, then popping up, rising slowly, adjusting my feet like I'm riding a skateboard. Not too far forward on the deck, and not too far back. But the whole time I'm practicing, I'm thinking about how she told the surf gods I was her *cute* friend, but *I* just told them she was my friend, instead of calling her *gorgeous*, or *beautiful*.

After half an hour of practicing the pop-up, my arms and shoulders are exhausted.

"Photo shoot!" Summer announces, and crawls to her bag, takes her phone from it. "Okay, stand on your board and face the shore."

"We're *on* the shore."

"You know what I mean. Look at the snack shack."

I look at the snack shack.

"Adjust your feet or you'll go over the falls. You

might go over the falls anyway, but at least *look* like you're trying to ride a wave."

I put my left foot in front, parallel to my right, both straddling the spine and pointing to the side. Knees bent, like I'm between sitting and standing.

She raises her phone, the one that has no service plan and a cracked screen.

"Now look determined. But happy."

I smile. I hold the pose. But Summer frowns and lowers the phone.

"This is no good. Your hair is dry." She looks around. "Don't move."

I do move, just a little, standing straight as I watch Summer borrow a sandcastle bucket from a kid nearby. She dips it in a wave that rolls in to accommodate her. As she turns back toward me, she reaches down for a clump of seaweed, then runs to my side.

I look at the little yellow bucket. "Are you planning on dumping that water on my head?"

She dumps the seawater on my head. "Am I *what*?"

I wait for the water to fall past my face, then open my eyes. She's grinning. She raises the seaweed and drapes it from my hair, across my face.

"Seriously?"

"Oh, this is gonna be epic." She arranges the seaweed, curls it around my eye, across my cheekbone.

She backs away and raises her phone. "Bend your knees." She squints my way. "Watch out for the waders who've strayed into the surf zone. Now pretend there's a shark."

My arms fall to my sides. "You said the Big Kahuna scared them away."

"He did. Well, the one he punched, anyway." She sees my dismay. "Okay, no sharks. Pretend there's a depth charge."

"A what?"

"Never mind. Just keep smiling, like you're riding the best wave ever. Great. One more." She lowers her phone. "Perfect."

I stand straight. I pull the seaweed from my hair and face. "Will you send me those pictures?" I'm thinking I'll show them to Fern, if she'll ever talk to me again.

"I can't," Summer says. She reaches down for her bag, and drops her phone inside. "Remember? No service plan."

"Ugh. Why don't you have a plan?" As soon as it comes out of my mouth I regret it. Maybe money is too tight in her family? But she seems to spend money pretty freely.

Then Summer turns from me to face the shore. She stares out at the waves, past the waves, past everything. She solemnly marches down to the smooth, wet sand. Bending down, she writes something with her index finger, moving to her right as she forms the big words. Then she turns back toward me and pauses on her way to her beach bag, her board.

"I never wanna see another text message," she says.

I reach for her but I'm too slow. She's already passed by. So I look toward the water's edge as a wave comes in and washes away the words written in the sand— washes them away so she never has to see them again.

Hurry home! Hank is hurt.

20

THE NEXT DAY we're out past the break zone, in the calm beyond the place where the waves originate. Swells roll beneath us, heading toward the beach, but they don't break until they've left us behind. I'm face-down on Summer's pink surfboard. She's beside me on Hank's, sea-foam green.

"Okay," she says. "Show me your pop-up. Here comes the wave."

I look out to sea.

"Not really," she says. "We're just practicing."

I look at my hands gripping the rails, which is the surfer word for the sides of the board. "Are my hands good?"

Summer shakes her head. "Hanging on to the rails is perfect when you're boogie boarding, and when you're duck diving through waves on your surfboard, or paddling out to the break zone. But remember that to pop up on your surfboard, you start with your hands flat on the board beneath your ribs, head peeled up to admire the beach you're about to land on, then spring up to a crouch, all in the blink of an eye."

I sigh. Then I take a deep breath, flatten my palms beneath my ribs, and quickly push myself up. But the deck squirts out from under me and I fall back into the water. My board would have flown away if it weren't leashed to my ankle.

"Good try," she says. "Toes to the nose just a little bit more. Bring your left foot a little further forward and make sure your balance is good before you rise."

"I'm *trying.*"

"I know you are. You're doing great. And remember, you can't catch a wave without falling off a few times first."

"I know, I know."

I pull myself back on the board, again and again.

Again and again my imbalance throws me off.

"I think I've got the falling-off part figured out."

"One more try," she says. "Almost there."

I don't believe her, but I do it anyway. I flatten my palms beneath my ribs, then arc them, and this time I feel like instead of bringing my knees and feet forward to get my left foot in front, I'm dragging the board back toward me. I land on my feet, fully crouched, then unbend myself just a little.

I can't believe it. I'm standing on a surfboard in the middle of the ocean. The continent kneels before me.

"Betty!" she shouts. "You did it!"

I grin, then look down at my feet. My left foot is in front, my right foot is in back. They look like they're ready for action.

Then the board squirts away from me and I drop with a plunk into the deep water.

Summer laughs. I laugh too, because now I *know* I can do this. I did it once, I can do it again.

I do until my arms and shoulders are exhausted.

"Smell that?" Summer asks. "That offshore wind is making the waves mushy, and it's also advertising the treats of the snack bar. I'm ready for a portobello burger." She breathes deeply into her nose. "And onion rings."

That sounds really good. *But.* "Aren't we gonna try to catch a wave first?"

She smiles. "Really? Haven't you had enough for today? 'Cause I'm starving just from watching you fall off your board."

I splash her. "Can't we just try one? I mean, we're heading in anyway, right?"

"You have a point. And I like your spirit. So, remember that it's very much like boogie boarding. Paddle forward when it comes so you're as close to the speed of the wave as you can be. That gives you a bigger window to catch it. Then, right when the wave is pushing at your feet, you pop up. Ideally you're on top, right on the lip, and then you drop down the front and angle into it. Which is very much like bending your way into a turn on a skateboard."

"Got it."

"Really?"

"Heck yeah." I try to sound brave.

Summer smiles. "Okay, Betty, let's see what you've learned."

We paddle in, facedown, toward the impact zone. We go slowly, until we're at just the spot she's looking for.

"Okay. See how the wave made a face right there? Its back is to us, but the faces should show themselves pretty consistently at this spot. So if we start right here, maybe even back up a bit, then we can paddle into them and pop up right on top." She looks over her shoulder at the swells. "Ready?"

I nod.

She turns from me and paddles away so that we aren't close enough to crash into each other. She gives me a shaka, and I shaka back at her. I watch as she observes the ridges of baby waves coming at us. With each wave she looks at me and shakes her head, until the one when she doesn't.

"Catch it!" she shouts. She starts paddling in, looking like a cat stalking a bird, and I follow her lead. I take a last glance to my left just as I feel the wave behind me. I press off the deck and pop up.

It feels right. For a split second I see the shore in front of me. But then the view tilts, somersaults, and I plunge headlong over the nose of my board, into the water.

The wave crushes me. My forehead hits the sandy bottom, my nose fills with burning salt water. It drags me along, holding me down. I can feel my board's leash, tugging at my ankle.

This is how it will end, like I knew it would. It started with getting my feet wet. It ends on the ocean floor, held down by the weight of trillions of gallons of salt water rolling over me like a freight train.

But the wave finally passes, and I push off the bottom and gasp for air as I break through the surface.

I cough uncontrollably as I pull myself onto my deck. I stay low, hugging it tight, then begin kicking feebly toward the shore.

Another wave breaks over me, and I fall off the

board again. I'm struggling to climb back on when Summer reaches me.

"Are you okay? Are you okay?" She looks panicked. "Oh no! Your head!" Her eyes search my hairline. "What's my name? Do you know my name?"

"Summer."

She kicks alongside, watching me. The beach draws near.

"And you? What's your name? Do you remember?"

I smile, then drop off the board onto my feet in the shallow water. "I'm Betty," I say.

Summer smiles grimly. "Yes. You certainly are." She hurries along beside me.

I fall to the dry beach. Summer drops beside me and unleashes me from my board. The sand is warm, but I'm shivering with the wind coming off the sea. Salty snot hangs from my face. I hack and cough, and spit up a mouth full of goo. Beneath me there's a tiny sand crab that I'm pretty sure just came out of my mouth.

"Lie on your side," Summer says. "Keep coughing." She stands and waves at the lifeguard shack with both arms.

I keep trying to cough. My head is killing me. I stare down at the sand, but in a moment I see athletic, tanned guy legs and red lifeguard shorts.

"What happened?" It's a deep voice.

"We were doing a party wave," Summer answers. "She went over the falls and banged her head on the bottom. I looked over my shoulder and saw her tombstone bobbing. She was in the spin cycle for a while."

"Can you look up?" he asks, kneeling down. "Let me see your eyes."

I do. I see the face of Jack, Summer's favorite lifeguard.

"Ouch," Summer says.

Jack grimaces. "You got beat down pretty well." It's more of a lifeguard diagnosis than a medical assessment, but it sounds about right. "How does your head feel?"

"Throbbing." I cough, then throw up a little, which is rather embarrassing.

Jack stands up straight. He waves at the lifeguard hut, does some sort of hand signals. "Protocol says you should get to the hack shack. You're doing a lot of coughing. And you got a gnarly blow to the coconut. Better to have them make sure your puffers are clear and that you don't have a concussion."

"I'll go with you," Summer says. She looks spooked.

"Where are we going?"

"The hack shack," Jack answers. "The emergency room."

I shake my head. "I can't go there."

"You *have* to," Summer says.

I look at her, and this time I see the girl whose big brother hit his head, and now—

"Okay," I say. I reach to Summer. "Stay with me?"

"I won't leave you."

Summer strokes my right arm until it almost hurts, but I don't tell her it almost hurts. Jack stays with us, one eye on me and one on the beach. Two more lifeguards come around.

The lifeguard ambulance arrives. It has thick, wide tires for the sand. It looks like a beach toy. They strap me to a stretcher that's like a board. They say they want to keep my neck from bending since I hit my head on the ocean floor. Jack takes our surfboards, says he'll keep them in the lifeguard shack.

The lifeguard ambulance brings me to the sidewalk and the street, and then they unload me and put me in the regular kind of ambulance you see everywhere. Summer tells the paramedics that I'm her sister so she can ride with me. The lifeguards know Summer and they know she isn't my sister but they don't tell the paramedics it's not true.

I'm strapped in the back. Summer sits above me, still stroking my arm.

They blast the siren, which feels oddly unnecessary. Through the windows, from my back, I see open sky.

218

Then we hit the streets and I see condominium towers and streetlights and trees.

I close my eyes. When I open them we're at a hospital. The back door of the ambulance opens. Summer trots alongside as they roll me into the emergency room.

They take me right into a little room with curtains for walls. Summer and the paramedic from the ambulance answer questions from a nurse. Two people in white outfits slide me off the board and onto an adjustable bed.

Something that feels like a clothespin pinches my index finger. Summer pulls a sheet up over me. Suddenly I remember I'm wearing a shorty.

"What's your name?" a young nurse asks. She's wearing SpongeBob SquarePants scrubs.

"Betty."

"Her real name is Juillet," Summer says, "but I call her Betty."

The nurse smiles. "Do you know where you are?"

"The hack shack."

The nurse smiles again. She looks like maybe she knows how to surf, with strong shoulders like you get from paddling out, and highlights in her hair. She looks at the monitors, and so do I. I know from my mom being a doctor that I'm not absorbing as much oxygen as I should be. I feel like a starfish is about to crawl out of my lungs.

"The doctor will be right in," she says.

I push myself up in the bed. I feel grains of sand beneath me, trapped between the bare skin of my legs and the cool sheets. Summer moves in and holds my hand. I cough once, into my hand, which brings on a whole fit of coughing. I look in my palm but there's no starfish.

"Okay, let's see what we have here." It's a familiar voice. I shrink beneath the sheet as my mom walks in with a half dozen ducklings—doctor interns—in tow. She picks up the clipboard with the chart.

"Okay," she begins, reading from the clipboard. "Female, twelve years old. Blow to the head and seawater in her lungs. We'll give a listen to her lungs and do imaging on both areas. Concussion protocol and guarding against dry drowning, which you folks will see enough of if you end up working in hospitals this close to the beach."

Mom finally looks toward me, and her knees buckle in shock. The chart falls from her hands as she grabs hold of the counter to steady herself. An intern retrieves her clipboard. I avoid eye contact as she composes herself and moves in.

"Good afternoon, young lady." She's acting like she

doesn't even know me. Her fingertips trail over the throbbing pain of my forehead. "Can you tell me your name?"

"Betty."

Summer leans forward. "Her name is Juillet but I've been calling her Betty."

Summer doesn't know it's my mom—she must not recognize her from when she was in her swimsuit at Pinkie Promise on the day we first saw each other. But Mom is regarding Summer with amused curiosity. "Betty?"

One of the interns tips his head toward Mom. "That's surfer slang for an attractive surfer girl."

The numbers on the heart monitor get bigger, my pulse quickening. Summer's been calling me Betty all month and I had no idea it meant that.

Mom looks back to me. "Do you know where you are?"

"At the hack shack."

Again an intern leans in and interprets. "That's surfer slang for a hospital."

"And do you know why you're here?"

She won't act like she knows me, so I won't look her in the eyes. "I went over the falls and got drilled. Swallowed a Neptune cocktail."

Another intern leans to Mom, but she waves him

away. "I think I get the gist of it. Do you have any pain in your neck?"

I shake my head.

Mom reaches to me with both hands. She massages the back of my neck, the sides. The feel of her fingers against my skin makes me think my eyes will well up with tears, but I'm not gonna let it happen.

"Any soreness here? Or here?"

I shake my head.

Her hands withdraw from my skin. "Sit up for me and take a deep breath." She unzips my shorty to expose my back. The stethoscope is cold against my skin. "Again. Once more, nice and deep." She zips me back up, takes a step away. "Well, she doesn't appear to be in any danger. First let's get her feet up and her head down below her lungs. There's some fluid in there, so that'll help drain it. Then Tylenol and an ice pack for her crown, scans for her head and lungs, just to rule out anything serious." The interns nod, make notes on their own clipboards.

The foot of my bed rises, the head lowers. Immediately it feels like my lungs are a shampoo bottle tipped upside down to get the last shower's worth.

Mom hands orders to the nurse, who leaves. Then she addresses the interns. "Everybody take five. I'll meet you in the break room." The interns nod, scatter.

Mom watches them go, then pulls the curtain shut and sits in a chair beside my bed.

"You gave me quite a surprise."

I won't look at her. "You acted like you didn't even know me. Just another set of vitals."

Mom clears her throat. "Well, protocol dictates that when a doctor cares deeply about a patient, they should allow another physician to administer treatment. I wanted to be the one to care for you, so I pretended not to know you."

"This is your mom?" Summer's eyes are big. "I didn't recognize you in the hack-shack threads!"

Mom smiles. "You must be Summer."

"I'm so sorry this happened," Summer says. "Betty—I mean Juillet—has been learning so much. She's really a strong swimmer. Maybe I shouldn't be trying to—"

"You're fine," Mom interrupts. "Thank you so much for getting her here."

"Summer's practically a lifeguard," I say.

"I believe it," Mom says.

"So . . . will you still let Juillet hang out with me?" Summer asks.

Mom gives Summer a curious look. "Of course. Really, thank you for looking after her." She puts her hand on Summer's shoulder. "I'm assuming you girls told the paramedics you're sisters?" Summer smiles sheepishly, says nothing. "If you'd like to stay with Juillet during her imaging, I'll get a Lyft for us to go home afterward."

"Yes, please," Summer says.

After the imaging, after Mom discharges me, the three of us ride back to Fourth Street together. Summer and Mom chat like besties while I sulk, an ice pack against my forehead. The Lyft drops us at the cottage, and Summer says good-bye, says she'll go back to the lifeguard shack for our boards.

Inside the cottage, the light is mellow in the front room. I lie on the couch, and the breeze and the sound of occasional cars on Fourth Street through the open windows lull me to sleep.

When I open my eyes, Mom is kneeling beside me. The sun has gone down but the light has not yet faded from the cottage.

"How do you feel?"

I think about it for a moment. "Stupid."

Mom's hand strokes the hair away from my forehead. At first it seems like she's just stroking her daughter's hair, but then I realize it's because she's a doctor and she's looking at my forehead because I'm a random person with an injury.

"There's some aloe on the patio. I'll get you some to

help prevent scarring on this forehead abrasion."

She rises to her feet, walks toward the door.

"I didn't want to go to the ER." I say it rather loudly.

She pauses. "Well, I'm glad you did."

I cover my eyes with my arm. "If you think I took a dive onto the ocean floor and nearly drowned just so I could have a reason to finally see my mother on this stupid vacation, then you're wrong."

She stands there, quietly. "I'm not accusing you of that."

"I would have asked to go to a different hospital if I'd known we were going to the one you're working at."

She clears her throat. She sounds thirsty when she speaks. "I thought it was understood that I would be quite busy during this visit. I've enjoyed being able to spend some time with you, but I am spending most of my time working and at the conference."

She's still. Somehow I know her face is tilted down. Then it turns up my way again. "When you came in, it was like I barely recognized you. You looked so healthy. All that playing in the sun and the water. And your *speech*." I can hear the smile in her voice, and I lift my arm to see it. "It's like you're a different girl. A *surfer* girl."

"I haven't caught a wave yet. A wave has obviously

caught me, but I haven't caught *it*."

"Well," she says, "I just felt so *proud* of you."

I stand and walk quickly to my bedroom, close the door behind me. I look out the open back window. In the distance, over the roofs and trees, down the slope, is the sea. You cannot see it, but you can feel it on the breeze.

I walk back into the front room. Mom is still standing in the same spot on the hardwood floor.

"Why did you feel proud of me?" I ask.

She looks up at me. "I just couldn't believe this beautiful, adventurous young woman was the same girl I came to Ocean Park with a few weeks ago. You've grown so, so much."

I go back into my bedroom, closing the door more quietly this time.

I like what Mom said.

I open the desk drawer, and stare down at the list of goals.

More exercise and fresh air.
Confront your fears.
Go outside your comfort zone!
MAKE A NEW FRIEND
LEARN TO SURF?
FIX FERN THING

GET CLOSER TO MOM

HELP SUMMER LIKE SHE HAS HELPED ME

The list keeps getting longer, but maybe that's good. 'Cause while the list is getting longer, I'm getting stronger.

I close the drawer, then step toward the open window. I take a deep breath, turn my left foot outward, and assume the warrior pose. I bend into it, and I feel it—my strength, my balance, preparing for my eventual wave.

21

THE NEXT DAY, Summer and I are walking up the hill, skateboards under our arms. We've been at it again with the skateboard lessons, as Summer thinks the better I am at not falling off a skateboard, the better I'll get at not falling off a surfboard.

It's too steep to ride up the hill to Fourth Street, and I'm tired from our riding up and down the boardwalk all day.

Summer is in one of her quiet moods, which she's been drifting into more and more of late. At least it isn't as mysterious as it was before I met Hank. And I'm relieved at feeling pretty sure it isn't because of something I've done or said, but thinking this, I feel guilty for being happy that it's not about me. Because what it *is* about is much more serious or important than whatever I am.

We turn the corner onto Fourth Street, and reach the driveway leading to Summer's house. She stops.

"Do you wanna see something?" She says it with a weariness.

I nod. I wanna see something.

She leads me down the driveway pavers to the door. Inside, the house is quiet. I follow her up the stairs to the second floor. Behind Hank's door his day nurse, Maria, is singing in Spanish. But Summer leads me the other way down the short hallway, past the elevator to another closed door, which has her name spelled out with letters cut from aqua-blue construction paper. She puts her hand on the doorknob but pauses. She speaks quietly and without humor.

"Don't laugh. Don't make fun. Don't judge."

I shake my head. "Never."

The door swings open, revealing her world, a world I can only love. The walls are covered with posters from surfing magazines, everything blue and aqua blue and ocean blue, and sea-foam green and golden sun. A pink surfboard ruined by teeth marks hangs above her open window, which frames her beloved Pacific, quiet in the distance.

But Summer is kneeling at the foot of her bed, pulling a shoebox from beneath it. She sits on the bed and motions for me to sit beside her. As I do, a photo catches my eye, in a frame on the nightstand. It's Summer, maybe two or three years ago, standing beside a boy who must be Hank, the way he looked when he was full of life, athletic and handsome. They're on the beach, grinning, standing beside their surfboards.

"It's not like it's the only thing that's important to me," she says.

I look from the photo to her face. "Surfing?"

She nods. "I'm not, like, totally one-dimensional."

"Of course not," I say. "But if you were, it'd be a case of you choosing really well."

"Or it chose me." She twists her lips, like she's thinking of her fate.

"What's in the box?" I ask.

"Just . . ." She can't seem to finish her thought. So she takes the lid off and sets it aside.

The box is nearly empty. Just a few seashells laid across the bottom.

"May I?" I ask. She nods.

I remove the dry, beige form of a seahorse and hold it in my hand. It's only as big as a cricket. Attached to it with a bread-loaf twist tie is a tiny plastic cowboy with a lasso, riding it.

A hummingbird darts through the open window and hovers above me, as if he's curious about the contents of the box. He nods, satisfied, then zips back out the window into the open sky.

I put the seahorse back in the box and remove a sand dollar that's bigger than a silver dollar. It's more the size of a silver-dollar pancake, but with its tiny design imprinted on it.

There is also a perfect crab claw, bleached white by the sun.

A few shells too perfect and rare to find on any beach.

A tooth that obviously came from a shark, maybe even left behind in the flesh of Summer's butt when she was attacked.

A piece of light blue sea glass, which I lift and hold against the light of the window.

"That's the color of the sea when I dream of the sea," she says.

One item in the box I do not touch—a lock of hair, held in a small plastic bag. It's the same golden color as Summer's, but I know it isn't Summer's.

Each object is a story, but a story Summer isn't able to tell. Not with her voice, anyway.

I realize how dearly I wish to be associated with something in the box. Like, *here's the sand crab you threw up when you wiped out.* Or *here's the bottle cap you stepped on.* Immediately I feel guilty for wanting to be in the box. I don't feel like I could be associated with an object holy enough to belong in there. *Here's your name printed on a grain of rice in a minuscule jar with a tiny cork on top.*

"I'm sorry I kept Hank a secret for so long," she says.

I put the sea glass back into the box. "It's okay. I understand."

"So that's it. My box of secrets." She looks from the box to the open window. "I'll try not to keep any more secrets from you."

"Me too," I say. As I say it, I wonder what my secrets are, and whether they're as bright and beautiful as Summer's.

Later, in bed but not yet asleep, I think again about the box beneath Summer's bed, imagining stories for each shell and object inside. I also wonder why I don't have such a box myself. And I think about what Summer would put in the shoebox if she lived in Lakeshore instead of Ocean Park. I decide it would contain arrowheads and dead bugs and snail shells. She'd be a lake skater and a tree climber.

I make a mental note that I will become these things

when I get back to Lakeshore. I will *return* to being these things. Skater of frozen lakes, climber of trees. I did these things when I was younger, before Dad left, and I can do them again.

As I drift off to sleep, I wonder whether I'll still feel this way in the morning—or, rather, a week from now when I'm back in Lakeshore. Whether I'll still feel this brave without a fearless girl to show me the way.

22

I WAKE TO see Mom standing over my bed, smiling placidly.

I sit up. "What?"

She's wearing her I'm-enjoying-myself clothes—a summer dress with the straps of her one-piece bathing suit visible on her shoulders. "Nothing."

"Why are you here?"

She sits on the edge of my bed. "I'm not going into the hospital today. Remember?"

"No." My thoughts turn suspicious. "Are you just doing this because of me wiping out yesterday?"

She shakes her head. "That was two days ago. And this has been on the calendar all along."

"Oh."

"So we get to spend the whole day together."

I think about this. I decide against reminding her that last time we were supposed to have the whole day together, she ditched me before lunch. "I'll have to tell Summer. We're supposed to ignore alien orders at ten."

"I'd love to ignore alien orders with the two of you, whatever that means. It would be nice to meet Summer under more pleasant circumstances."

I smile weakly. Mom leaves the room, and I sit up, wondering how it will be to share Summer with her.

The smell of waffles toasting gets me out of bed. It was nice of her to start the waffles, but while I eat, Mom sits at the table reading something having to do with the hospital. Even on her day off she can't leave it alone.

"So what is all this about disobeying aliens?" She's looking at me over her glasses.

"Ignore alien orders," I reply. "You'll see."

A short while later, Mom and I are shuffling down the sidewalk with our beach gear. She's as pale as I was on the second of July, wearing sunglasses with lenses as big as drink coasters, and her flip-flops smack the sidewalk with every step.

"There," I say, pointing down.

Mom looks at the section of sidewalk in front of us. "'Ignore alien orders.'" She pushes her shades back up on her nose. "So what do we do?"

"We wait. It's just our meeting place." I look away from her and her sunblock-white nose and bug-eye shades. I look across the street at the Big Kahuna's bungalow, where a surfboard leans beside the door.

In a moment Summer appears down the block. Even from a hundred yards, and behind shades, it still looks like she's squinting, as if she's wondering whether I'm really standing next to my mom. But she's smiling, and I become aware of my heart beating, and the sweat on my palms. Maybe I'm nervous about how Mom will treat Summer after the emergency room. What if she really does blame her for what happened?

"Hey, Betty!" Summer says as she arrives. "Hey, Betty's mom! It's good to see you again!"

"Please," Mom says, reaching out her hand. "Call me Abbie."

Summer ignores Mom's hand, instead handing me the two surfboards and giving Mom a hug. Then she takes a step back. "Call me Summer!"

I watch their expressions. Apparently I'm the only one worried about their regard for each other after the emergency-room fiasco.

Mom raises her beach bag as if to reveal her intentions. "I was hoping I could tag along today."

Summer grins at me, then at Mom. "Awesome! Do

you surf? Never mind. Are you okay with getting in the water, then? Betty's made huge strides." Her eyes get big and she punches me in the shoulder, then looks back to Mom. "We can teach you to boogie board!"

Mom gets this excited look like she's a little girl, and wiggles back and forth where she stands. It's totally embarrassing.

But in a matter of minutes we've switched out the surfboards for boogie boards and are walking down the hill on Ocean Park Boulevard. Summer seems to have forgotten about me. Everything she says is meant for my mom.

"We can rent you a boogie board next to the snack shack. Do you have money? What am I saying, of course you have money. And when we're done we can show you the eats we've been feasting on at the snack shack. Which is really much more than a shack. Do you like onion rings?"

"Why, yes—"

"And then lots of times we stop for a scoop at Pinkie Promise after we leave the beach. Do you remember seeing me there on your first day in town?"

"Yes, I—"

"I was behind you and Betty in line. You guys looked so cute together! And then I saw you both going into the cottage right down the block from my house and

I've been hanging around Betty ever since!"

We're now standing at the stoplight at Main Street. I'm staring at Summer, because it's strange to hear her tell it this way, from her point of view. Even knowing she put the postcard in our door, I never would have had the nerve to imagine that Summer had put any effort into our being together, that it had ever been anything but accidental.

We unload down at the water's edge, spread out our towels. Mom slathers herself with sunscreen in preparation for our sponge board session. I'm wearing my shorty, so there's very little of me that needs sunscreen, and I'm quite a bit darker than when we arrived here on the first of July.

Once we're out there, Mom is a natural. Apparently any skills I have I inherited from her. She catches a wave on her first try, and rides like eight out of the first ten perfectly. She and Summer are having the time of their lives. I'm getting more and more furious with Mom. Maybe because I feel like she's stealing my friend, and also because the day she said she'd spend with me she's spending with Summer instead. But she doesn't even notice.

"Are you having fun?" Mom asks. She's in the middle of our lineup, with me on her right and Summer on the other side of her.

"This is just wonderful." I give her a fake smile.

Mom smiles back, then looks over her shoulder at a wave that isn't right. I'd ride it away from her, from them, if it could be ridden. But it can't be ridden, and I don't want to look bad trying.

"I'm supposed to FaceTime with Dad and Genevieve later," I say. It comes from nowhere. It isn't even true.

Mom doesn't respond, but she isn't grinning anymore. She looks again over her shoulder at the next rise.

"What do you suppose he sees in her?" I ask. "I mean, she's beautiful and everything, but she's kind of an idiot."

Mom doesn't look happy. "Is there a reason you're bringing up your dad and that woman right now?"

I shake my head. "No. It's just she's apparently really good at this kind of thing."

"Bomb!" Summer shouts. I'm pretty sure I know what she means by *bomb*. But I'm looking at Mom looking at me.

"Are you intentionally trying to hurt me?" she asks.

Before I can answer, a giant wave breaks on top of us. It smashes me down and drags me along the bottom. Under the water the roar is angry. A thousand bubbles cry as they rise. Finally the wave lets go of me and the foam board strapped to my wrist as it moves on, and I break to the surface. I gasp for air.

Then Mom pops up beside her board, hair in her face, coughing. She begins paddling blindly toward the shore. Her board is loose, and she leaves it behind as she swims toward the beach.

"Mom!"

She doesn't answer, but keeps swimming, and coughing. I climb on my boogie board and kick toward her.

Of course Summer caught the wave and rode it in. And of course Summer meets Mom on her way back out before I do. She looks all concerned, and they walk side by side in the shallow water toward the sand. Meanwhile Mom's board bumps me, but I ignore it. It can drift to sea and she can forfeit the rental deposit for all I care.

But I go in anyway, more because I'm done than because of caring about anyone.

When I reach them, they're sitting on the towels. Summer is watching Mom shiver. She puts my towel over Mom's shoulders.

"She'll be okay," Summer says. She looks at my expression, then rises to her feet. "I'm gonna get her board."

I turn to watch Summer jog off toward the runaway board, which is bouncing on the rakers in the shallows. I turn back to Mom.

"You got crushed."

Mom nods.

"Worked."

She nods again.

"Had." I stare down at her. "That's how it felt when Dad left."

She looks up at me, shields her eyes from the sun.

"Over the falls," I say. "Into the spin cycle."

She shakes her head. "Him leaving felt worse."

"Really?" I glance over my shoulder to Summer, who has Mom's board under her arm. She watches us from the water's edge, then turns away and looks at the sea. "You never said a single thing about Dad leaving."

"Didn't I?" She shakes her head. "Maybe I was trying too hard to look like I was strong."

She doesn't seem at all doctorly at this moment. She doesn't look like she could save lives. Instead she looks like a shipwrecked woman.

"Sorry I was being mean." It occurs to me I wanted to see her cry for what happened more than a year ago.

"Sorry for everything I've done wrong," she says.

I don't want her to feel that way. I really don't.

"Maybe," I begin, "you just didn't have a chance to come up for a breath yet."

She smiles a tiny smile at this.

I sit beside her. "How about on the count of three we both take a big breath?" I don't know where this brilliant idea came from. But it really is brilliant. "Like we've been dragged along the bottom, but the killer wave has passed, and we're finally coming up for air."

She nods. "Sounds like it's just what I need."

"But you gotta gulp at it like you mean it. Like you've been wanting it for forever."

"I will." Now she looks like she'll cry. "I have."

"Me too." I put my hand on her knee. "Okay. One, two, three!"

We both gasp loudly, like we've broken through the surface after rising from the darkest depths. We're so loud we scare away a seagull, whose wings beat a breeze as he takes off. A baby on a blanket to our right starts crying. I put my head down and laugh into my palm.

Mom laughs too, then puts her arm around me. Seeing her laugh is way better than making her cry.

At the water's edge, Summer is backlit by the descending sun. From the darkness of her silhouette her smile flashes.

Everything feels perfect in this moment.

"I missed the piano recital on purpose because I didn't think I could bear playing without Dad being in the front row." I just kinda blurt it out.

I feel Mom's eyes on me, but she doesn't say anything.

"I blamed it on Fern because I didn't want to admit to feeling that way. I didn't want Dad to be able to make me so sad. I didn't want him to be able to ruin my life. Especially since he's supposed to love me."

"I understand." She stares into the distance. "And he does love you."

"Can I tell Fern I'm sorry?"

"Of course." Mom nods. "You can say anything you'd like."

"And I want to say I'm sorry to you, too. For lying."

"Apology accepted. And circumstances understood."

"I'm so sorry."

She's silent for a moment. So am I. Summer kicks at the waves, glances over her shoulder at me and Mom. She gives us our moment.

"We should talk about our pain more," Mom says. "Whenever it enters our hearts."

"But not right now," I say.

"Not right now," Mom agrees.

I catch a glimpse of Mom's feet, which are beginning to look rosy. "You should put some sunscreen on those," I say, and reach into the beach bag.

23

I'M DREAMING OF the ocean. It's the color of the sea glass in the box beneath Summer's bed, the same color she dreams it. I fell asleep with the pull of the waves rocking me to sleep, and all night I'm there. But it's a bright, endless beach with nobody on it—only me—and the waves push and tug, push and tug.

The tugging wakes me. I open my eyes and see a hand extended through the dark open window, the white curtains, tugging my arm.

"Betty!" comes the urgent whisper.

I sit up, pull the curtains across the window to reveal Summer's excited face.

"I'm so glad you didn't scream!" she says.

I rub my eyes. "I'm kinda surprised I didn't."

"I need your help. Get your shorty on, quick! I won't look."

I'm so tired. I tug the curtain back across the window and stand. I hear the curtain screech on the rod again, and turn to see Summer's anxious face.

"Did you shut it for privacy or because you don't wanna help me?"

"Privacy. Gimme a minute."

She smiles and pulls it shut again. I drop away my jammies and head into the bathroom, where my short wet suit hangs in the shower. It's still slightly damp, and not comfy to be putting on at four in the morning.

"Hurry!" she whispers as I return to the bedroom. "Do you wanna climb through the window?"

I hadn't pictured myself leaving the house that way, but now that she asks, there's something about it that sounds adventurously appealing. Summer backs away from the window as I put my head through and look down. The ground looks clear and soft. I hand her my towel, open the window as far as it can go, and put through one leg, then another, then make the short drop to the ground.

"Come on!" she says, leading me alongside the cottage.

"Where are we going?"

We reach the sidewalk and turn toward her house. "You'll see."

The neighborhood is quiet at this hour. No cars pass on Fourth Street in the short time it takes to walk to her house. She tiptoes up the pavers to her door. I follow. On the porch she puts her finger to her lips. "We can't wake up my mom," she whispers, then opens the door.

We sneak-foot up the stairs and across the landing to Hank's door. This is when I get scared.

"What are we doing?" I whisper.

"We're rescuing Hank!" She opens his door and creeps in. I don't want to be left behind, so I go after her. A wheelchair is beside his bed.

"We're gonna lift him into the wheelchair. I'll get him under his arms and you get his legs. On the count of three, okay? One, two, three."

He's light, and his body is lifeless like a sack of potatoes—but a sack of potatoes that's half empty—as we move him to the wheelchair and arrange him in a sitting position. Summer straps him in, first across his chest and then at his ankles.

"He weighs barely anything," she says, hands on hips. "He's fifteen. He's supposed to be the one able to carry *me*." Summer lays a note on Hank's pillow, then gets behind the wheelchair. "Come on, to the elevator.

Close Hank's door behind you. *Quietly.*"

Summer cringes when the elevator dings. We take it to the bottom, and I open the front door in front of her. There's a ramp built of unpainted wood to lead us off the porch.

"Grab my board," Summer says, motioning over her shoulder.

I notice it for the first time, leaning against the porch rail. I carry it under my arm and follow her down the pavers to the sidewalk.

"Where are we going?"

"Dawn patrol, obviously."

A shiver runs down my spine. I'm afraid but thrilled. Down Hill Street we go, with me in front of the wheelchair just in case. Every few steps I look back to make sure I haven't gotten too far ahead.

"Is this legal?"

"Of course! He's my brother. My mom would kill me. But this is gonna be great."

"Are you gonna make him surf?"

I sense that the wheelchair is no longer rolling along behind. I turn and see Summer with her head down, her golden hair almost touching the sidewalk, trying to control her laughter. Finally her face reappears.

"*No*, Hank isn't gonna surf. But he would if I'd let him." She begins rolling the wheelchair downhill again. "He's gonna watch."

Though I'm pretty sure Hank can't see, I feel somewhat better with this picture in mind. She'd joked about duct-taping me to her skateboard to get me through Third Street when it was too scary for me, so the picture of Hank strapped to a surfboard was presenting itself in my mind.

Main Street is empty as we cross. So are Neilson and Barnard. Then we reach the sand. Immediately it's clear that the wheelchair, with its skinny wheels, wasn't made for this. It won't roll at all.

"Dang it!" Summer gazes across the sand at the dark ocean, where ghostly bits of fog drift from the surface as they near the beach. There are a couple of figures visible in the water.

A growly voice sounds behind us. "Need a hand?"

We turn and see an old guy in a wet suit. He's not old like nursing-home old, but his hair and beard are long and gray. Jabbing the nose of his surfboard into the sand, he looks strong in spite of his age.

"I'm trying to get my brother close to the water so he can watch me surf." She looks from the old guy to Hank. "He taught me how."

The old guy smiles. "And I taught Hank. At least I taught him everything I know. Then he became a regular hotdogger." He steps forward. "If you carry my board, I can carry your brother."

Summer smiles. "Thank you."

We watch as the old guy bends down, reaches under Hank's arms, and lifts him over his shoulder. "Come on, Hank. Let's catch some waves." He looks like a big, strong father carrying his child to bed.

Summer grabs the old guy's surfboard and we follow behind. Hank's wispy hair bounces as the man trudges in the sand.

A hundred steps and we're at the water's edge. Summer scratches her head. "Maybe he could sit up against you, Betty? Do you mind?"

"Not at all."

I sit down in the sand, and the old guy lowers Hank and sets him against my raised knees. He's as feeble as a featherless baby bird. His ghostly feet rest in the sand.

Summer arranges his pajamaed legs in front of him. "Please make sure the brace keeps his head supported."

I nod. "I will."

She kneels down and fastens the top button of Hank's pajama shirt, then stands.

The old guy claps his hands together. "It's gonna be epic this morning." He leashes his board to his ankle. "Waves like corduroy."

Summer turns to him and smiles. "That's why we're here for dawn patrol." She looks down at Hank. "Also because this is kind of a kidnapping and we needed to do it while my mom's asleep. Thank you so much for being an accomplice."

"Anytime." He picks up his board and jogs into the surf.

Summer watches him leave, then looks to me and smiles. "*That*," she says, "was the Big Kahuna."

My eyes follow the old guy attacking the waves. A major shiver runs down my spine.

I feel like I've just seen a mythical creature. It occurs to me that I doubted his existence until just now, seeing him.

This stupid surfing thing keeps getting more and more amazing.

Then Summer gets on her knees in the sand before Hank. She leans close, her forehead pressed against his, and speaks so quietly I can barely hear.

"It's a big surf this morning, Brother. I know you can hear it." She looks over her shoulder at the waves. "I know you can *feel* it." She squeezes his shoulder. "I'll catch one for you."

Then she leashes her board to her ankle, picks it

up, and runs at the ocean. She dives into it, paddling away from me and Hank. Then she reappears in the distance, among the rising white mists on the black ocean, knees on her pink board, facing the beach. The Big Kahuna is to her left. Summer looks at him, then glances over her shoulder at a rising swell. I watch as she drops to her belly and paddles forward, then pops into a crouch on a wave that comes to life beneath her and continues to grow as she shoots down the front of it, then curls to her right.

I may not know much of anything about surfing, but I know she got it just right. She's so far out, and the waves are so noisy, but I swear I can hear her happiness as she rides it.

"It's your sister, Hank," I hear myself saying, a lump in my throat. "She's destroying it."

As the light grows in the eastern sky, giving an eerie shimmer to the fog sliding off the waves, Summer pops up and shreds the waves again and again. It's absolutely sick. After each wave caught, she grins and shakas at Hank and me from the shallows, then turns and heads back to the break zone for another ride. I watch her and learn until I can almost picture myself doing it.

Finally she drags her board onto the beach and

unleashes herself. She bends down at the water's edge and picks up a length of seaweed, fresh from the salt water. She works at it as she approaches, fashioning it into a wreath. As the sun peeks over the horizon, she kneels beside Hank and ties it around his head.

"My surf prince." She kisses his cheek.

Summer sits beside Hank, holding his limp hand, facing the waves. Then she leans her head on his bony shoulder, and for a while I'm just a silent prop, there to keep Hank from falling back. And I'm totally okay with it, I'm so much more than okay with it, with watching this, being present to witness this.

The ocean sends its breezes, the waves crash, the seagulls cry.

The wisps of fog dissipate.

An old woman with rolled-up jeans searches for shells at the water's edge.

Then the first shift of lifeguards arrives, six of them in red shorts and white T-shirts, who will spread to the lifeguard shacks up and down the beach. They come to us. They know Summer, and they know Hank, and they talk to him like he can hear them. They're surfers with jobs, but mainly they're surfers, kidding him, even though Hank can't hear their jokes. He couldn't laugh anyway, and neither can they, not really.

Finally they slide Hank onto a surfboard and lift him at the count of three, 'cause that's how lifeguards do it. They look like pallbearers as they carry him to his wheelchair, away from the ocean, away from the surf.

24

IT'S JULY 28, and I still haven't caught a wave. Summer and I have been at it for three hours today, and I'm wiped out from wiping out. I'm noodle-armed from soaking in the miso, popping up and falling off. Finally I feel defeated.

"Let's pig out at the snack shack," Summer says as we walk from the water. "It's an important part of the training program."

I smile half-heartedly. We stuff our towels in our beach bags and head away from the shore, boards under our arms.

As our feet leave the sand and hit the sidewalk, we see that there's a line at the snack shack. We claim a table with our boards, and head toward the counter.

"Uh-oh," Summer says, stopping short.

"What?" I follow her gaze to the two boys standing at the back of the line. It's the two jerks we saw on the Fourth of July, and again at the party at the Big Kahuna's. The two jerks we can't seem to get rid of. *"Oh."*

Summer stands straight. "Come on. I'm sick of avoiding them. Let's get this fight over with." She leads me to the end of the queue, directly behind the boys.

I'm nervous, worried about what might happen, what mean things they might say. But as we stand behind them, as I observe them, the boys look smaller than they did on the Fourth, or at the party. They both have the same skater haircut, which suddenly seems like a sign of their insecurity. Both sets of skinny legs poke from baggy shorts and end at their checkered Vans. Each holds a skateboard.

We stand there for a moment before Summer pokes the taller one in the back. He turns to face us, as does his friend.

"Oh, *you*," he says to Summer with a sneer. Then he looks me up and down. "Nice job breathing life into the corpse." He says it nastily. He must be referring to my punk-Goth look melting away in the sun and surf.

"Hey, appropriately named *Wade*," Summer says. "I just wanted you to know that I forgive you for being one of a zillion guys who suddenly started showing interest in me when Hank went into a coma." She turns to the side and spits on the pavement to show her disgust. The quieter boy looks down at the spit like he's afraid it'll come to life. "It was super classy of you to only have the courage to get in my hair after my big brother could no longer watch over me."

Wade looks stricken. "I—"

"And I don't really care that you're goofy-footed. It's more that you suck and you're a kook."

Wade's mouth hangs open, eyes glassy. He turns away awkwardly.

The friend looks from Summer to me. He furrows his brow, then turns and stares up at the menu board.

Summer glances from side to side, then lifts her chin to face the menu. She doesn't look like she's deciding what to eat. Nor does she look triumphant, like she just slayed a bully or whatever.

I look at the menu board, since everyone else is, then at the back of the taller boy. *Wade.* He moves his skateboard from his right arm to his left, then back to his right. He has a woven-thread friendship bracelet on his left wrist. Maybe he made it for himself. Or someone across the ocean in China made it and he bought it at a tourist shop, the kind Mom would find charming.

"Wanna split some onion rings?" Summer asks dejectedly.

I nod. "Sure."

I look behind me. There's nobody there. We're still the last in the queue.

I look up in the sky as though I expect something to be there. But it's just the sky.

Finally Wade and his friend have ordered and left the counter, and it's our turn.

Summer steps up. "Yo. Onion rings, please. And a mango smoothie for me."

"Coconut for me," I say.

"Hey, Summer." The girl at the counter rings us up. "Ten bucks."

Summer frowns. "Did you get both our smoothie orders?"

The girl nods. "Yep."

"And the onion rings?"

"*He* paid for the onion rings." She nods toward the tables. "The taller kid. I guess he knows your jam."

"Oh." Summer fumbles with some dollars. I give her mine.

We pay, and tip the plastic jar, which says *cool people tip*. Summer is quiet as we wait for our food, and as we stop by the condiment station for ketchup and hot sauce and napkins. She's lost in her thoughts as she fills up five, six little cups of ketchup, putting a bit of hot sauce on top of each. She reaches for a seventh.

"Maybe that's enough?" I ask.

Summer doesn't answer, but puts the empty cup back on the stack. She stares at the tray in front of her, then grabs a few napkins from the dispenser. She closes her eyes, holds them shut for a moment. Tightly. Then she turns suddenly toward the tables. I hurry by her side, a smoothie in each hand.

There's one open table where we stowed our boards, but Summer veers with determination toward the one the boys are sitting at, beneath a big umbrella, just off the sidewalk in the sand. I stay by her side.

The boys look up. Summer stands stiffly with the tray held in front of her.

"*Two*," she says, addressing Wade, "it was nice of you to buy the O-rings. And *one*, I'm sorry for what I said about you being a sucky kook and appropriately named. And all the other trash talk I've been slinging the past several months."

The friend, the shorter one, clears his throat. "*Appropriately named* was actually pretty solid."

Wade throws half a french fry at him.

"And," Summer says, "you're absolutely sick on the sidewalks. Maybe sometime you could pass along some tips."

"Likewise with you and the waves," Wade says. "You are most definitely Hank's sister."

Wade's words cause the tray in Summer's hand to tilt, almost spilling the basket of onion rings and all the little ketchup cups, which slide toward the front of it. Fortunately I'm holding both smoothies, one in each hand.

"That's, like, the most righteous thing anyone's ever said to me." Summer looks down, levels the tray. "Well. Thanks for the grub. Hang loose."

Wade gives the shaka. His friend does too. I raise a smoothie to them both, which seems silly somehow. Like it's less cool than the shaka. But I guess someone needs to be holding the smoothies.

We turn to leave, but Summer stops and looks back at the boys. "Also, it was solid of you to try to be a friend to me after Hank got hurt. I guess I just wasn't ready."

Wade furrows his brow and nods like it's cool and it's no problem. But he looks overcome with emotion. Like he's gonna cry any second.

As I sit with Summer at our table, the onion rings taste so real they bring tears to my eyes. I also finally understand fully why Summer puts hot sauce in the ketchup. It's just like everything else about her—wanting the most excitement, the most adventure from everything. Wanting whatever is the opposite of being in a vegetative state. As I think of this, our fingers bump, reaching for the same onion ring at the same moment.

"Yours," she says, and waits.

"No, yours."

Summer smiles, but her eyes are glossy. She takes the onion ring, dips, eats. I stop watching her and take one for myself.

"What just happened?" I ask. "With Wade?"

Summer shakes her head. "Hank was always cool to everybody. He *is* always cool to everybody." The half-eaten onion ring dangles from her fingers as she stares across the sand, across the ocean. "But boys my age have always been intimidated by him because he's a legend on the waves. Best junior surfer in SoCal. Then when he got hurt, a bunch of them started coming around, acting all friendly to me. I couldn't tell if they were just being nice or whether they were trying to . . ." Summer sighs. "I don't know. Make me their girlfriend or whatever. And I hated both possibilities, because they only started talking to me because Hank was . . ."

Gone. Summer doesn't finish the sentence, but that's what I hear in my head. She dips the rest of the onion ring in the ketchup and hot sauce, puts it in her mouth.

"It wasn't their fault, what happened to Hank," she

says. "But I hated them anyway." She reaches for her smoothie, and looks to me with hopeless eyes. "Who's gonna watch over me now?"

All I can do is reach my hand to hers. I wish I could say *I will watch over you,* but in three days, I'll be gone.

25

EXHAUSTED FROM A morning picking up garbage on the sand with the Beachcombers and an afternoon chasing waves, Summer and I walk from the shore to Main Street, surfboards under our arms. I may look more like a legit surfer with darker skin, stronger limbs, and natural highlights in my hair, but I still haven't caught a wave. I've gotten as far as popping up properly and seeing the shoreline in front of me lots of times, but when it comes to the drop, I always wipe out. Sometimes the wave slips away from me and sometimes I fall in front of it and get crushed, but I never get it right. I'm trying not to let Summer see how discouraged I feel, but I'm running out of time.

The list of goals in the drawer is noisy in my head. I've made progress on almost all of them, but this goal has no shades of gray. When I'm home in Michigan and looking back at my month in Ocean Park, either I caught a wave or I didn't.

It's the twenty-ninth of July, and everything is about to end.

I flash a smile at Otis as we walk inside Pinkie Promise, 'cause that's the new me. He doesn't ask me if I caught a wave. Not just because he's helping a family of obvious tourists in front of us, but also 'cause he's asked a few times already, and he knows he'll hear it from me if I do. He'll be able to see it on my face.

When it's our turn to order, Summer looks into the case at the featured flavors while I look at her. The light from inside the refrigerated display shines off her eyes. Though we're indoors, her golden hair flashes as she pushes it behind the ear facing me. Her skin glows as though the sun were trapped beneath it.

There are only eight flavors every day, which is one of the things I like about this place. I don't have to go completely crazy making up my mind.

Summer looks into the case and tilts her head. "The pistachio looks sad."

She's right—only a little pistachio remains, chased to the corners of the container.

Behind the counter, Otis clears his throat. I look at him, and he's looking back at me.

"The pistachio is bummed out because summer's almost gone," he says.

I feel like he's talking about me, that I'm the pistachio and Summer is the summer. It's weird to compare my feelings to pistachio ice cream, but that's what it feels like.

Summer nods like she's come to a decision after extensive deliberation. "Then I'll have the pistachio. To cheer it up."

Otis smiles and begins scooping.

"With whipped cream," she adds.

"You got it, Chiefette."

Then Summer turns to me. She looks happy.

"Pistachio is the flavor you ordered when I first saw you," she says. "Way back on the first of July."

"You *remember*," I say.

"Of *course*. Do you remember what I had?"

I think for a moment. "You were behind me. So I was already outside eating mine when you got yours."

Summer smiles, kind of a disappointed smile. But I feel like she knows I'm not really telling the truth. Because I *do* remember. I remember her coming outside holding her cup, and I remember that it was cherries jubilee, with whipped cream and a maraschino cherry on top, and that she tilted her head to bite at the whipped cream, then saw me watching her, and smiled.

Otis gives Summer her pistachio. The lights of her eyes shine brighter.

"How about you?" Otis asks.

"The same, please."

Otis goes to work scooping mine. I turn to Summer and watch her take the cherry off the top.

"These bear little resemblance to actual cherries," she says, and bites it from the stem. "Like they've been sent away to fake camp and returned as candy."

I smile. At her voice, at her words. At her.

"Do you wanna eat it on the bench outside?" she asks.

"Sure."

I look from her to Otis, who holds my pistachio at arm's length. I take it from him.

"On the house today," he says. "Since you brought happiness to some sad pistachio."

Summer puts her hands on the counter and leans forward. "I love you, Otis." Then she turns and beckons me to follow her.

"Thanks, Otis," I say.

We pass through the door of the little shop and onto the sidewalk of Main Street. We sit on the bench against the window.

"Cheers," Summer says, holding her cup to mine.

"Cheers," I say. We tap cups.

We eat and watch everything move past in the cool breeze—a letter carrier with a canvas bag over his shoulder, who waves at Otis but has nothing for him, and cars, and a family holding boogie boards under their arms, and a tiny dog on a leash walking beside a woman who looks unhappy behind her designer sunglasses.

I eat my way through the whipped cream to the pistachio. It's so good. It's so good it makes me sad. And I hate that something can be so good it makes me feel sad.

"I'm gonna ask Otis for more whipped cream," Summer says. "Are you in?"

I frown. "It's kinda mean to use your charm to get something free from him."

Summer gives me a smile like I'm kooky. "Charm? Otis is, like, practically a man. And all he cares about is surfing anyway. But I really *do* love him. He's a peach."

"Whatever." I poke my ice cream with the spoon. "No thanks."

She stands. "Be right back."

I don't watch her as she turns to go inside, 'cause it's weird to be constantly staring at her. Instead I watch a Big Blue Bus pass on its way down to Venice. Then I see a homeless man stoop over a garbage can and take a paper bag out, look inside it, then drop it back in the can.

I notice that the light of day is weaker than it was when I arrived. The days are growing fewer. They are almost gone.

Summer breaks the spell of melancholy as she comes through the door. "Score!" She sits beside me on the bench, her depleted ice cream renewed with a ridiculously high tower of whipped cream. I watch her take a bite. Again she doesn't use a spoon, and it's left all over her mouth. She licks some of it away.

"Is there a place like this where you live?" she asks. She turns to me, and I glance across to the sunny side of Main Street.

"Not as cool as this." I look back at her. I watch as she uses her spoon now to dig at the pistachio, taking a little whipped cream with it.

"You know what makes this place so great?" She taps her cup with the spoon. "Besides Otis and extra whipped cream, and the deliciousness, and how it's a perfect way to reinvigorate yourself after an afternoon getting crushed by waves?"

I feed myself another bite, and shake my head. I look at my suntanned bare feet, resting on either side of a cigarette butt on the sidewalk. I'm listening, waiting, but Summer doesn't say anything, so finally I look at her. She's smiling at me.

"Wait." She reaches into her canvas bag and takes out her phone. She taps the cracked screen a few times, then turns it around to face me.

"What am I looking at?"

"Her. She's the reason this place is so great."

I take the phone from her and zoom in to the picture. It's some girl on the beach. Her hair is wet and laced with a strand of seaweed, draped across her face. She's laughing. I'm guessing she just rode a sick wave and got crushed. Good for her. I hope she choked on a Neptune cocktail.

I shrug and hand the phone to Summer. "Who is she?"

Summer puts her fanned-out hand on her chest, her eyes and mouth gaping. "Are you kidding me?"

I shake my head.

"Look again." She passes the phone back.

I stare at the girl in the picture. She looks supremely happy, wild and careless. Her eyes are as green as the seaweed that hangs across her open mouth. Her teeth shine brilliantly.

It's totally annoying.

Then my eye catches a mole over the girl's lip. I zoom in.

I turn her around in my mind: It's above her lip on the left, slightly raised.

My free hand rises to my own lips, the left side. My fingertip finds the small, raised black mark.

"It's you, Betty. *You* make this the best ice cream shop ever."

The feeling is too much, Summer saying this wonderful thing about me, and the phone falls from my hand. I turn away from her, but she puts her hand on my shoulder and turns me back. She's laughing. I move my sunglasses from my hair to my eyes.

"Let me see!" she says. She reaches for the shades, takes them away. She searches my eyes, back and forth, like there's something hidden behind them.

I try to keep from smiling too much, but I'm smiling too much. And I try to keep from crying, because I don't want her to know how happy I am. I try to keep from looking away, but I couldn't turn from her now anyway, because I'm like a flower feasting on her radiance, even though that doesn't sound like a very good poem, or at the very least it needs some work. But at least I'm not afraid of it for resembling a poem anymore.

I want to say something back, but I can't think of what. So I look from her eyes to her lips, because there's a bit of whipped cream on the upper one.

"Anyway," she finally says, "maybe we could see a movie on the promenade tonight? Or we could drink tea and write postcards to each other?"

But I feel paralyzed. Maybe worse, like the undertow is knocking me off my feet. Or I've gotten sucked into a rip current and I'm being pulled out to sea. To dangerous waters.

She gives me a curious look. "Are you okay?"

I can't answer, but my face comes toward hers, in slow motion. I know my face is moving toward hers because her eyes are getting larger, and the bit of whipped cream is getting bigger, and whipped cream definitely doesn't just *grow* under any circumstances I'm aware of. And I feel like I'm dreaming as the bit of whipped cream, which has begun melting against the backdrop of her upper lip, gets nearer my own mouth, until—noses bumping—I can taste it.

The sound of a car alarm down the block wakes me from my trance. Then my face backs away from the lips where the whipped cream had been, and I see all of Summer. She has a look on her face I have not seen before.

Surprise? Amusement?

"What was *that*?"

The dreamy feeling is gone. In its place is my hammering heart, a suffocating sense of dread.

"I—because you had whipped cream on your lip?" It comes out like a question, like I'm presenting it as a theory.

Summer laughs.

Then I completely freak out. My cup of ice cream is knocked to the sidewalk as I bolt from the bench. I trip on some dog's leash, I fall but get up and keep running. My knee burns from the sidewalk, my mind is in disarray as I run across Main Street on a red signal. Up the hill, hearing my feet slap the pavement, dragging my burning lungs, until I reach the sidewalk on Fourth Street and jump over *Ignore Alien Orders* and run inside our cottage and into my bedroom, and slam the window shut for I don't know what reason, then lie with my face in my pillow and wonder what I've done.

As my breathing slows, my eyes still pressed to the pillow, it occurs to me—she did not follow, she did not call after me, she did not run after me. She just let me go.

It's a relief.

It's heartbreaking.

I don't know what it is.

26

THE NEXT MORNING, I wake way too early. I don't want to face the day, because I'm equally afraid of two possibilities. In the first scenario, I see Summer and she asks what the heck I meant by what I did. In the second, Summer avoids me and I'm left remorseful and wondering what the heck I meant by what I did.

I sit in the living room, the light and the breeze filtering through the white blinds. I put the Beach Boys on to try to cheer myself, but instead it makes me sad.

I sit and replay in my head what happened, to see if I can figure out what went wrong.

It wasn't the whipped cream. Whipped cream is never an ingredient of the apocalypse. Whipped cream is delicious, and even if it's a little weird to take it from someone else's lips with your own, there are stranger and worse things than that.

It's all because of my feet. My stupid feet carrying me away. My feet are supposed to do that when confronted with a giant tsunami, or a shark if a shark happens to appear on dry sand. My feet are supposed to act that way if I'm being chased by zombies, even though everyone acquainted with the genre knows zombies are never in much of a hurry.

Summer might have believed me when I told her it wasn't a kiss, but rather just a whipped-cream thing. But then my feet gave me away.

My feet didn't even give me a chance to think, or to tell Summer she's the best friend ever, the best *everything* ever. But maybe there's more to it than that. Like a secret I've been keeping even from myself.

Sitting in the empty cottage, thinking these things a day too late, I hear a skateboard coming down the sidewalk, and my heart leaps. *Da-duh, da-duh, da-duh.* But it keeps on going. *Da-duh, da-duh, da-duh.* I run to the door, and out past the tall hedge to the sidewalk. Looking down Fourth Street, I see it's just a guy on a skateboard with a sponge strapped to his back, making the turn to go down Ocean Park Boulevard.

Coming back to the cottage, I see a postcard stuck in the screen door, and I run to it. I don't know how

I could have missed it when I came outside. I pull it from the screen—but it's just a coupon for Gino's Pizza. Dejected, I go inside and stare at cartoons on the TV while the Beach Boys play in the background.

At five minutes to ten I walk outside to ignore alien orders. I feel like an idiot standing at this spot, because I feel sure she won't be joining me. So I bend down to tie my shoes so I'll look like I have a reason to be here. I unlace one, tie it, and begin doing the same with the other. As I do, I hear the sound of a man talking loudly. It's a guy coming down the sidewalk, arguing with himself, shouting and waving his arms. I stand, then move quickly to the cottage, my one untied shoelace flapping beneath me. I duck behind the hedge, and watch and listen as he approaches.

"The raccoons took my figs!" he shouts. "Shady-eyed devils!"

Hiding behind the hedge, I see his suit coat and pants as he passes. He's even wearing black shoes. But his suit is dusty and wrinkled, his face is sunburned, and his hair is greasy. He looks exactly the way people will look on day five after the apocalypse. The civilized world ends and they walk out of their offices, wearing the business attire they've put on for the last time, and hit the sidewalks. There are no pizzas to order, no running water. The toilets back up, the garbage gathers.

They wander the sidewalks in their obsolete attire, getting dirtier and more sunburned until hunger or thirst or zombies—or raccoons—finish them off.

It's a one-man apocalypse for this guy, who looks like he just lost his mind. The rest of the world hasn't ended yet, but it's ended for this guy. All the hobos, all the homeless people, start this way. Someone waits for them to come home and they don't. In a week they're beyond recognition. From then on they sit at the bus stop, but when the bus comes they tell it to just keep going. From then on they're fighting raccoons for their breakfast.

I walk back out to the sidewalk and go the opposite direction from the guy in the apocalypse suit.

This is day one of *my* apocalypse. This is how the end begins for me.

At five after ten I walk past the place in the sidewalk, ignoring alien orders as I do, and glance at Summer's house at the back of its lot as I go by. I don't want to knock on her door because I'm afraid I'll be unwelcome. If she wanted to see me, she'd be ignoring alien orders. I take a right on Hill Street, walk downhill for twenty steps, then turn around and come back like I've forgotten something. I casually glance at her house like it's something I haven't noticed before, like I'm not even aware of who lives there, and I ignore alien orders again, almost without thinking. Summer still isn't there.

I take a left at Ocean Park Boulevard and head down the hill. I slap the Third Street sign as I pass, angry at it for ever messing with me, angry at Mistress Scarfia for putting it in my head. Then I go into the library, walk through it, smile at Joe the librarian, walk out. Down to Main Street, where I walk up and down, peeking in the doors of the boutiques, the bookstore. I catch sight of my reflection in the toystore window, slowly raise my hand to my face. I'm decked out in full Goth regalia, from the dark curtains of my eyelashes to my black high-tops with skulls and crossbones. I have no recollection of applying the pale foundation, the ivory powder, the black eyeliner, the black eye shadow. I must have done it in a dream, or a nightmare. I must have done it to win Summer back, to win her like I did on day one. Or I did it because there is no hope of winning her back.

I double back down the sidewalk and enter Pinkie Promise. Otis isn't working. The owner, an old guy behind the counter, smiles. I tell him raccoons took my money. Then I leave.

I go back up the hill and stop in the little market on Fourth Street where Summer and I sometimes go for waters or snacks. There are only two aisles, so it doesn't take long to see she isn't there. But the Big Kahuna is, standing in line at the register. His long hair is messy, he's barefoot, his eyes are hidden behind shades. He nods at me with just the ghost of a smile. I smile back, but I don't think it's convincing. As I squeeze past, I note that he is buying rye bread and bananas and toilet paper, and one avocado.

This isn't how it's supposed to end. But I guess this is the end I've been preparing for, the end where something stupid and entirely unnecessary ruins everything that was good and wonderful. Not a tsunami or a meteor or zombies digging themselves out of their graves. Instead, my own stupid feet carrying me away when I wanted to stay.

In the afternoon I'm sitting in front of the cottage in the patio area when my phone lights up. It's Dad, FaceTiming me. I'm too mad to talk to him, but I pick it up anyway.

"Hello, Juillet!" He's wearing a robe.

"What's on your face?"

He puts his fingertip to his green cheek. "Oh, it's a beauty mask. I'm getting ready for bed."

I smirk. "I'm glad you called, 'cause I wanted to tell you I've given up piano."

His smile disappears. "You have?"

"Yeah. I'm gonna be a surfer instead."

"You learned to surf?"

"Yeah, I've been crushing it out here in Dogtown. But don't be disappointed I'm giving up piano. I mean, you're in Switzerland with your child bride, so it's not like you'd ever see me perform anyway."

His face hangs. The beauty mask cracks. "Juillet, I—"

"I'm giving up piano because it reminds me of you. I'm so mad at you for what you did to me and Mom. You ruined our lives."

"I'm sorry, Juillet. I don't know what happened, I—"

"I wasn't done needing you! You can't just decide one day to stop being my dad!"

I shout, "I hate you," but I shout it after disconnecting. Because I don't really hate him. I'm just so, *so* mad at him.

After my shout I'm left with the quiet of birds chirping, and the breeze moving through the hedge. I glance at my phone, but Dad isn't calling back.

I walk inside and through the cottage to my bedroom, and I take the list from the drawer. I write *DAD?* with the little pencil. Then I cross it out with a thick line dragged across the middle.

Mission accomplished. I told him how I feel, which is about all I *can* do. It's not what I would wish for. It's not him never doing what he did, or somehow everything being forgotten and going back to the way it was. But it's all I can do.

Mom gets home earlier than any day since we've been here, before it's even dark. She immediately recognizes that I'm depressed—mainly because of the Goth makeup—but she guesses it's because we're leaving. Which is part of it, but mainly it's because we're leaving and everything is ending badly.

Mom brought stir-fry from Main Street for dinner, and we eat it at the big table. It's the last supper, the end of summer, and Summer isn't here.

I'm going to miss this table. I'm going to miss this town. I'm going to miss ignoring alien orders, and the girl who taught me how.

The stir-fry looks like it hits all the right notes, but I cannot taste it.

Finally I set my fork down. I look across the big table, across the vast stretch of wood, at my mother. "How old were you when you had your first kiss?"

Mom looks up and wipes her mouth, her lips, with her napkin.

"My first kiss?" She does the thing with her eyes that people do when they're pretending that the answer is written on the ceiling. "In high school. Older than you." She reaches for her wineglass. "Why do you ask?"

"Just curious." I pick up my fork.

She takes a sip of her wine. "Did you meet a boy who makes you think of that?"

I smile just a little, but keep my eyes on my plate. "No."

"Well, you will one day."

I spear a snow pea. "I met a girl."

She looks up, swallows her bite. "Oh?"

"And we already did."

"Well." She takes another sip of wine. A little spills on her chin.

"Aren't you gonna say anything?"

She sits back, away from the table. "It's a bit surprising."

"That it was a girl?"

She doesn't answer right away. I can tell she's choosing her words carefully.

"I suppose if I'd thought of you kissing someone, I would have imagined it being a boy. But that's totally fine. I think mainly it's just surprising that my baby girl has had her first kiss."

"It was Summer."

She smiles now, a small smile that looks like it wants to be a bigger smile. She takes another sip of wine, then clears her throat. "Well, Summer is a lovely, charming girl. I can't imagine a better coconspirator for your first kiss."

I can't believe I've told her this. I wasn't even absolutely sure it *was* a kiss until I told her. It's like I needed to tell Mom I kissed Summer to be sure that's what I actually did. But I'm not gonna tell her that Summer *wasn't* a coconspirator, that she didn't kiss me back, that I ran away, that everything is ruined. And Mom can't seem to guess that my being miserable is connected to what I've told her.

"But," she adds, with a hint of an authoritative tone, "maybe that's enough for one summer."

It's *not* enough for one summer, for this summer, but it's all I'm gonna get of Summer.

After dinner, after cleaning the dishes we used for July and putting them in the cupboard, we walk down the hill. Mom turns to look at me with curiosity as we pass through Third Street. She gets an espresso on Main Street, and then we drop in for one last scoop at Pinkie Promise. Otis grins behind the counter as we enter.

"Good evening, ladies! Is this our good-bye?"

I can't seem to open my mouth, so Mom does. "Yes, we're flying out tomorrow."

Otis looks to me hopefully. "Will we see you again next summer?"

Everyone's staring at me. Like it's up to me to determine whether we'll come back next year, and whether Summer will ever go out on the ocean with me if we do. Instead I have a question of my own. "Have you seen Summer?"

Otis regards me for a second. "Have I seen Summer?" He smiles, then begins scooping my usual. "Well, I haven't seen Summer *today*. But over the past month, right about since the day you arrived—decked out very much like you are again tonight—I've seen Summer looking more like the happy, carefree girl I remember knowing before Hank's accident." He leans across the counter, offering me a cup of pistachio, staring at my eyes accusingly. "*That* Summer was missing for so long. And it's *so* good to have her back."

I smile back, but I'm sure I look like I'm gonna cry.

"And that's good news for the surfers of Ocean Park," Otis continues. "Because Summer may not know it yet, but she's the one. She's got the special sauce." He closes the case, comes around the front to wipe the counter with a rag. "Summer is the shaman of tomorrow. The priestess of the waves." He gets down on a knee, like he's kneeling to royalty. His head bows, messy blond hair hanging down, hiding his face. *The Big Kahuna.*

"Wow." The whisper escapes my lips.

Hearing Summer described this way—being reminded why I've felt so enchanted during the month of July—does not help keep my eyes dry while I'm hugging Otis good-bye. He hugs Mom, too. He makes me promise to keep practicing yoga, and to return next summer.

At least I can keep one of those promises.

When we get back to the cottage, I lie on the bed and stare at the ceiling in the room that soon won't be mine. I hear Mom packing in hers, and the thought of doing that myself is more than I can bear. This place that I never wanted to know, the suitcase I never wanted to unpack.

I drag myself off the bed and go to Mom's room. Her big suitcase is open, half filled with clothes. She turns from folding and looks to me.

"I tried so hard to learn to surf," I say. "But I never caught a wave."

She gives a sympathetic smile. "Maybe one day you will."

"Summer got bitten by a shark, right here." I turn to show her. "I've seen the scar. But she loves surfing so much she wanted to go right back out in the water."

"Really?"

"That was up by San Francisco. There's an old surfer guy called the Big Kahuna who keeps the sharks out of the Santa Monica Bay. He punches them in the nose."

She smiles bemusedly. "You don't say?"

"Yeah. He lives like three hundred feet from here. And you heard what Otis said. He says someday Summer will be the next Big Kahuna."

Mom stands with her barely used swimsuit in her hands. I stand with my arms at my sides.

"I *love* this place." Only after saying it do I feel it fully. "I don't want to leave."

Mom drops her swimsuit into her suitcase. "If you like it so much, maybe we can come back for a holiday next year. And you can be pen pals with Summer."

I smile grimly, because it won't be the same. It probably won't be for a whole month, and the girl I hung out with doesn't want to see me.

I pack everything except for what I'll wear tomorrow, and what I'm wearing to bed—my shorty. Wearing my shorty to bed is so pathetic it almost makes me hate myself. Wearing my shorty to bed reminds me of everything I wished for in the month of July and didn't get—the two things I wrote on the bottom of the list on the day I met Summer.

MAKE A NEW FRIEND
LEARN TO SURF?

Especially the thing I had and then lost, because of running away from the friend I made.

I'm sure I won't sleep, that I'll lie awake replaying my bad decision, feeling my remorse. But after brushing my teeth and lying down beneath this open window, with the fragrance of the sea and the hummingbird buffet washing over me, my body feels like the whole month has caught up to it. All of July spent running around, and swimming, and boogie boarding, and skateboarding, and trying to surf suddenly seizes me. It flattens me and tucks me in. I fall into sleep like an overstuffed beach bag dropped to the sand.

27

I DREAM OF a long shoreline, of a perfect day, with corduroy waves as shiny as melting ice.

And I dream of everything Summer taught me about recognizing the right wave, and how to paddle into it like a hobo jumping a train, and how to pop up, and how to curl against the drop like a parenthesis. I've never put this all together to catch a wave, but in the dream I do all of it perfectly.

But Summer isn't there to see me.

Then she *is* there, not in the dream but framed in the window, her arm reaching to me, her fingertips on my cheek. She draws her hand away as I sit up quickly, like I've been awake and waiting for her all night long. My heart accelerates, but not from surprise or fear.

"Thanks for not screaming." She's said this before, but this time her voice is sad. "So are you ready for dawn patrol or what?" She sounds unhappy, like she's mad at me.

I frown. "Obviously. Did you bring both boards?"

"Obviously."

I stand as Summer backs away from the window, then climb outside. Summer is holding the sea-foam-green board. I grab the pink board from where it's leaning against the house. We head to the sidewalk, then make our way down the hill on Ocean Park Boulevard.

The predawn is quiet as a postcard. No dogs bark, no crickets chirp, no cars go on the empty streets. No words are spoken between us. The only sound is the slap of our bare, calloused feet on the sidewalk.

I wish she would just get it over with and tell me it was weird of me to kiss her. Her keeping quiet is killing me.

She finally breaks the silence as we cross Main Street. "This is gonna be brutal."

I wait for further explanation, but it doesn't come. "The surf?"

"Yeah. The surf."

We make the last block and pass the little park with the playground equipment.

Then our toes hit the sand, and she speaks to it as we cross toward the water. "On a morning like this you might catch a wave and feel like you're on top of the world. Like everything is perfect and it's never gonna end. Then out of nowhere it ragdolls you. Next thing you know you're crawling on the sand, spewing up a Neptune cocktail, and you're done."

Again I listen for more, and again there isn't any. "The surf?" I ask.

She jams the nose of her board into the sand at the water's edge. "Everything." She kicks at a clump of seaweed. "Waves. Friends." Her gaze lifts toward the sea. "Hank dying."

My board falls from my hands, banging my ankle. "Hank died?"

Summer says nothing, but drops to the sand, falling on her butt like her legs have been cut from under her. My own legs are shaky as I lower myself beside her. I put my arm around her and pull her against me.

"That's why you didn't meet me yesterday?"

She nods.

I feel horrible. I was so selfish, being worried about myself when Hank's dying was the reason she was missing all day.

She gives me her hand, and I take it. We sit together watching the pounding surf, the white breakers appearing in the dark distance and rushing up to smash the empty beach.

"When I woke up yesterday morning he was already gone. I went into his room and my mom was lying beside him on his bed with her head on his shoulder. She didn't even have to tell me. I knew."

I picture it.

"Then I crowded in on the other side of Hank. We lay there telling stories about him for a couple hours. Mostly funny stories. Stories of his antics. And the *waves*." Summer turns to face me. "I told my mom how we kidnapped Hank and brought him to dawn patrol."

"What did she say about that?"

"She said she would have killed me if she'd found out." Summer laughs, then wipes her eyes. "But she was glad we did. She said she was sure Hank could feel it. The roar, the mist. And she said Hank would be watching every wave I ride for the rest of my life."

"He'll be riding with you." I nod, willing myself to believe it.

I believe it.

"Without you I could never have done it," she says. "Without you at my side these past few weeks, I would never have been brave enough to admit to myself what was coming for Hank. I never could have broken the rules of Hank's room. I never could have said a proper good-bye. And I never could have brought him to the beach at dawn patrol."

I can feel her eyes on me, but I can't look back. So I stare across the water and furrow my brow to keep from crying.

"Showing you my world reminded me how much I love it. And how much Hank loved it."

"I love it too," I say, my voice catching in my throat. A sandpiper advances on a retreating wave at the water's edge, then pecks at the wet sand.

Summer sighs. "These really are some pounders this morning. I mean, this could be a fun morning for an experienced surfer. But I shouldn't have brought you."

"It's my last chance," I say. Suddenly I realize how important it is for me to do this, how badly I want to catch a wave. Even just one. I need it the way Summer needed to bring Hank to his beloved shore one last time.

"But these waves are savage." She shakes her head. "You probably shouldn't go."

A coarse voice sounds from behind us. "Hank would go."

I know without turning that it's the Big Kahuna. And there he is again, tall and mythical in his wet suit, surfboard under his arm. He comes up alongside us and stands his stick in the sand. He appraises the scene before him, nods, and repeats it. "Yep. Hank would go." He bends to leash his board to his ankle and smiles at us, but the gentle sort of smile someone gives you when you're sitting on the beach, staring at the sea like everything you love has drifted away and you're hopelessly waiting for it to come back. Then he trudges off against the surf.

Summer watches the Big Kahuna leave. She's so close to crying. She's holding it in like a mouthful of water.

"Hank would go!" comes a friendly voice as Otis passes by in a full wetty. He shakas with his thumb and pinkie. Summer gives a sad smile, and shakas back at Otis. So do I, but he's already turned away.

"Hank would go!" A lifeguard in red trunks tips an imaginary hat to Summer as he heads out to catch some waves before his shift begins. Summer does the namaste bow to him, her hands joined together like a prayer.

It occurs to me that Hank is being paid the ultimate tribute. All the surfers know that one of their own is gone too soon. They know it like they know the surf report.

Gidget moves down the beach to find an open spot in the line. "Hank would most definitely go." She blows a kiss to Summer, who blows one back at her.

I feel a chill down my spine as the scene unfolds before me. All the experienced surfers know the precise moment when there's just enough light to read the waves. Dawn patrol is in full effect as a couple dozen dedicated surfers fan out on the empty water.

"Hank would go," I say, and rise to my feet. I bend down, hiding the emotion in my eyes from Summer as I leash myself to my board.

But Summer shakes her head. "I don't know if I can do this anymore." Her voice is choked with pain.

I kick at the sand. "I haven't gotten this close just to give up now. All month long you've been by my side when I was scared. Now it's your turn to let me help you." I turn away from Summer, to the angry sea. Then I reach down to her, offering my hand. "Take it."

Summer looks up. Then she reaches for my hand, and I lean back to pull her from the sand, to her feet.

"When we ride, we ride together." Again my voice cracks as I say it.

Summer stands straight, shoulders back, and faces the waves. "I'm most definitely Hank's sister." She nods at the dark, roiling sea. "And Hank would go." She wipes an eye with her palm, and bends to tie herself to her board. Then she rises, and finally smiles a smile that is more happy than sad. "We ride together."

My heart pounds as we run off into the ocean, ankle-deep like my first day, then waist-deep like my first week. We bounce over the incoming rakers, get pounded by the pounders and mashed by the beasts until we're out past the break zone, where the waves are born, bellies to our boards.

We pause to catch our breath. Then Summer turns to me, and my pink board bumps against hers, sea-foam green. "Are you ready?" she asks.

"Heck yeah," I say, trying to talk myself into feeling brave. But I really am ready, for whatever.

Then she furrows her brow and stares at the nose of her board. "Just in case you get crushed by a wave and I never get a chance to say this again, I want you to know I'm sorry I laughed when you did that thing with the whipped cream. When you said you were just getting it off my lips, I'm pretty sure I was hiding my disappointment. Because I was wishing it was a kiss."

I reach for Summer's board and tow her closer. "I only said that because I felt like an idiot."

Her eyes meet mine.

"It was definitely a kiss," I say.

"Oh," she replies.

Then the cunning Pacific pushes us even nearer each other, belly-down on our boards. Our faces are lined up, positioned perfectly, and I know it's gonna happen.

But before it can, a gigantic bluebird breaks right on top of us. We tumble off our boards into the sea, and come up for air, laughing, and her smile is back. *Summer* is back. It's all back.

"That wave was very rude," she says. We pull ourselves onto our decks. "If we're gonna catch a wave, we need a little distance between us so we don't crash." She paddles off a bit to my left, and turns. I face the shore in imitation of her.

But I'm thinking of the almost kiss. The ocean cast the spell, and then the ocean broke it, as carelessly as it plays tug-of-war with the shore. It's telling me I haven't earned it, that there's some unfinished business to take care of first.

Fine, then. Bring me my wave.

I look over my shoulder at a ridge rising in the dark water.

"Not this one," Summer says, and we let it go by, a wave that might have worked if we were a little closer to shore.

She looks back again, through the mists, toward Catalina, toward Hawaii, toward China. Then she looks at me, and shakes her head.

"Let it go."

We do. A wave I couldn't even see rolls beneath us, bobbing us as it goes.

I watch her, glance over my shoulder at the distance, and watch her again.

Mainly I watch her. I could watch her all day.

"Maybe we should move in a bit!" she shouts. Then adds, *"Wait."*

She studies the dark horizon intently.

Then she turns to me, eyes big.

"Akaw!"

"What?"

"Akaw! This one!"

I begin paddling when she begins paddling, but I feel it behind me, the swell, kissing my toes, and then beneath me, and I know I'm on my own.

My hands push me from the deck. I pop up.

My legs are strong, my feet are sure on the surface of the board, calloused from a month of walking barefoot on streets and sand. My stance is nearly perfect, and for a moment, perched atop the wave, I am Neptune's only daughter, surveying her domain. And then it happens, the drop, and I drop but I don't fall, leaning against the wave like I know what I'm doing, riding the sharp edge of the ocean, hearing noises coming from my body, through my mouth, of wildest happiness. I almost shout *cowabunga*, but I mustn't sound presumptuous on my first wave, however appropriate it might feel.

But I hear Summer shouting. She's shouting the very *best* words of affection and shouting my name, but she's calling me Juillet, and though she's calling me Juillet I feel like Betty, because I *am* Betty, I *am* the physically appealing surfer girl, strong and statue-worthy and still on this wave, still on this wave as it runs out of mojo. I have tamed it, what the wave has lost I have gained, and though I'm breathless I feel absolutely electrified.

In the thigh-high foam I bail from my deck like I'm jumping from a stage, and I grab my board and turn to Summer, who runs across the shallow water to me. Her eyes are as big as sand dollars—not little ones like the one she found for me, but full-size. She isn't saying anything, she *can't* say anything, because there are no words, not in this moment. There is a whole vocabulary and a catalog of song for it, for this feeling, for these feelings, for catching a wave and for knowing this girl, for *loving* this girl, but not in this moment. Instead she drops her board and puts her arms around me, and her head into my shoulder, and I put my arms around her and do the same.

The remnants of waves push, the undertow pulls. We hold the pose, we hold each other. Our boards tug at their leashes, urging us.

I don't want to let go of Summer. I don't want to

say good-bye. But somewhere above the blanket of the morning marine layer, the roar of a jet leaving LAX cuts through the sound of the surf, reminding me that I, too, must leave.

The sun will peek over the horizon, Mom will wake. She will know where I am, and who I am with, but still we must board—the entirely *wrong* sort of board—before noon, and leave Summer behind.

But not just yet.

"Another?" Summer asks.

"Another."

We say it again and again.

And next summer—if I have anything to say about it—we'll get back together and do it again.

Good-bye, California

WHEN WE FINALLY leave the beach there's no time to spare, so we run barefoot up the hill, boards under our arms. We turn the corner onto Fourth Street, jump over alien orders, and slip behind the hedge in front of the cottage. We pass through the screen door and find Mom just inside, arms folded. The suitcases are lined up by the big wooden table. My pair of flip-flops is on the floor, and a cover-up is draped over a chair.

"Sorry I'm late."

Mom looks at her watch, then speaks calmly. "There's a taxi coming. It should be here any minute." Her expression softens, her arms unfold. "We'll be fine. You're right on time."

"She caught a wave!" Summer beams. "Many, actually. Your daughter is quite sick."

Mom almost laughs at this. "Well, I'm very happy to hear that."

I look down at the bright pink surfboard I hold.

"I'll keep it for you," Summer says. "Nobody gets to ride it except Betty." She clears her throat. "By which I mean Juillet."

I pass the board to her.

A yellow butterfly flutters past the side window. I hear the tires of the yellow taxi on the driveway.

"Well," Summer says. "So long for now."

I look to Mom. She stares back. She keeps staring back, then suddenly snaps her fingers. "I'm just gonna go make sure I didn't leave anything in the medicine cabinet." She turns away and walks down the hall.

I take a step toward Summer. She leans the boards against the table. I tilt my face slightly as it moves closer to hers, so I don't bump her nose with mine, like I've got loads of experience with this kind of thing. Her lips touch mine, and I feel the warmth where we meet. Then her hand takes mine, guiding it upward to her heart. She holds it there, and I can feel the pounding against my fingertips. Like her heart wants to come home with me.

There's a pounding on the screen door. We pull away from each other as Mom's footsteps return down the hall. "That's our ride."

Eyes shining, Summer looks radiant as she turns from me and steps toward Mom.

"It was nice to meet you, Maja."

Mom smiles. *"Abbie.* And it was lovely meeting you, Summer."

"Okay, Maja." Summer moves in, hugs Mom, then draws back. "Thanks for bringing Betty into my world." Then she takes my hand, squeezes it, and turns away. She gathers the two surfboards under her arm and smiles over her shoulder as she walks out the door. Her golden hair flashes across the window, and she is gone.

I listen to Summer's footsteps disappear. I sigh. "Thank you for checking the medicine cabinet."

Mom turns to me. "Happy birthday," she says. Suddenly she looks happy and relaxed, like maybe she did have a bit of a holiday after all.

Sitting on the airplane, I look through the window at the tarmac and the big jets from every continent as we roll back from the gate to get in line for takeoff. There's a little green bug with transparent wings on the window, the outer layer of glass. He hangs tough as the ground crew pulls away and the jet begins to slowly taxi down the runway.

"*Maja*," Mom says. She's looking at her iPhone. "According to *Bro-man Bob's Surf Dictionary*, a Maja is 'a tight surfer mom.'" She sounds amused.

"Yep."

Mom extends her hand to me. "From your desk drawer." She holds a slip of paper. It's the list of goals she wrote for me on our second day, with the items I added. I take it from her, revisit it.

More exercise and fresh air.
Confront your fears.
Go outside your comfort zone!
MAKE A NEW FRIEND
LEARN TO SURF?
FIX FERN THING
GET CLOSER TO MOM
HELP SUMMER LIKE SHE HAS HELPED ME
~~DAD?~~

As I read the list, I check off most of the items in my head.

I have been transformed by fresh air and exercise.

I have faced my fears, both real and imaginary.

I have gone outside my comfort zone and into the break zone, where I have learned to surf, and caught a wave beside the best and most complete friend I've ever known.

"Regarding 'get closer to Mom.'" Mom powers off her phone and puts it away. "I've been thinking."

"What?"

She takes a pull on the straw of the iced coffee she brought on the plane. "I don't know how you'd feel about having me around more, but that's what I'd like."

"What do you mean?"

"You know. Around the house. And around you." She takes another sip. "Spending less time at the hospital."

I frown. "Is this because you're suddenly worried about how I might turn out?"

She gets this look like she's sad for me for thinking that. But she puts her hand on my arm and smiles.

"No. It's because I'm excited for how you *are* turning out."

I smile back at her. "That'd be epic." It really would be.

The flight attendants stand in the aisle, demonstrating the safety instructions. But my mind is elsewhere. I fish in my backpack for the postcard I wrote to Fern and never sent—the one where I confessed to blaming her for my missing the piano recital. I take a picture of

it with my cell phone while Mom busies herself find-
ing the crossword in the airplane magazine. Then I
open a text message to Fern and attach the picture to
these words:

> I'm on an airplane, about to take off. Coming home. Here
> is a postcard I wrote and never sent to you.

I pause, thumb poised.

I close my eyes and think of all the difficult things
I've done in the past month. All the brave things.
The daunting list, nearly conquered. Then my poised
thumb lowers to the screen. *Send.*

I wait half a minute before I can see Fern is writing
a response. Finally it comes through.

> OMG I HATE YOU

I feel my brow furrow, and I turn my phone away
from my eyes. I knew that was coming, and I totally
deserved it.

Staring out the window at the Hollywood Hills, I
see a jet racing down the runway. The little bug on my
window is positioning himself, getting ready for his
pop-up.

My phone buzzes again. I turn it slowly to face me.

I FORGIVE YOU! YES TO ADVENTURES! CAN'T WAIT
TO SEE YOU!

Tears roll down my cheeks as I text back a blubber-
ing series of happy emojis. Then I switch my phone to
airplane mode and wipe my eyes with my arm. I turn
to Mom.

"When we get back to Lakeshore, I'd like to be
friends with Fern again."

Mom watches me, waits for more.

"But it's gonna be different," I say. "I don't wanna
hang out at the mall consulting with Mistress Scarfia. I
wanna have adventures. I wanna paddle in a canoe, and
climb trees. I wanna swim in the lake, and skate on the
pond in winter. I wanna get mosquito bites and poison
ivy. Or at least be somewhere that it's a possibility."

Mom smiles. "That sounds . . . epic."

"It wasn't Fern's fault I wasn't doing all of that
before. The woods have been there. The lake has been
there. And they're still there."

Mom looks like she's gonna melt.

"There's something else. Dad FaceTimed me yesterday afternoon."

"He did?"

"He was getting ready for bed. He had a beauty
mask on his face."

Mom covers her laugh with her hand.

"I told him I was giving up piano and that instead I was gonna surf."

"You're giving up piano?"

"No. I just said it to try to hurt him. I also lied and said I had caught tons of waves."

Mom smiles. "Well, you did catch tons of waves this morning. Maybe it was more of a premonition than a lie."

"I told him that I wasn't done needing him to be my dad, and that I was mad at him for ruining our lives. Then I hung up on him."

Mom looks stunned. But I can tell she feels like I struck a blow for her, too.

"Well," she says, "I guess the ball is in his court. But I'm proud of you for speaking your mind. I think you were right to scratch that item off your list."

I smile. The list is the first thing I'll put into the box I'll keep all my future treasures in. This list, and the tiny sand dollar Summer found and gave to me.

This realization feels exactly like a wave has crested suddenly, splashing my face. But a happy wave, the kind that greets you as you paddle out for another epic ride.

I have to turn away from Mom because I'm feeling too much at once. I've cried so much this month, tears that were overdue. But some of them have been the best kind of tears. Because I've felt so much. *Grown* so much, like Mom said.

I look again at the bright window, at the little bug, and the little bug looks back. I give him a shaka. I'm sure he'd shaka back if he could, but he's hanging on for dear life at this point. And I know how *that* feels.

The airplane does a U-turn, moving my view away from the Hollywood sign on the distant green hills.

The engines get noisy. We speed down the runway, picking up speed. The little bug trembles on the window.

"*Bluebird,*" I whisper.

The little bug pops up and soars from the window. He's left behind, shredding the current, but I'm sure it's the ride of his life. Maybe he'll fall in love with the feeling, and hop back up on another ride so he can do it again.

Faster and faster the jet roars down the runway, then tilts and lifts, until we can no longer feel the pavement beneath us.

Good-bye, California.

Almost immediately we're over the ocean, and my view is to the south. Through the broken clouds rising from the dissipated morning marine layer, I see pleasure boats, and an oil tanker down by the refineries. I look straight out to sea at the deep blue, and wonder at all the life it holds.

Seaweed. Men in gray suits. Sand dollars that are sometimes more like sand dimes.

Then we do another U-turn, this one in the sky, angling to the left. Soon we're back over the continent. Past my shoulder I can see the coast, the pier at Santa Monica, and just before it the beach at Ocean Park.

Somewhere below, Summer is probably getting dressed in something other than a swimsuit, to spend the day with family who are in town for Hank's funeral in a couple of days. Maybe I'm wrong about Summer changing out of her swimsuit. Maybe they'll have Hank's funeral in beach attire. They really should. Maybe Hank will be buried with his surfboard. Or maybe Summer will continue riding it.

Suddenly I realize I never told Mom about Hank, or about Hank dying. I glance at her, smiling at the inflight magazine. This moment, up in the sky, doesn't seem like the right moment to tell her.

What if Mom would let me go to Hank's funeral, if Summer invited me? This airplane isn't gonna turn around and go back. But what if Mom let me fly back whenever the funeral is?

I sigh, and look back through the window. Also down there is Pinkie Promise, where Otis will soon begin his shift, scooping pistachio and cherries jubilee, and flirting with Betties.

In his bungalow on Fourth Street, the Big Kahuna is probably resting after his long morning surf. The Big Kahuna I leave behind isn't the one I saw buying toilet paper at the little market on Fourth Street. Instead it's the Big Kahuna who made the best guacamole I ever tasted, who carried Hank over his shoulder, bringing him to the shore for the very last time. This Big Kahuna is probably taking a nap, or maybe waxing his boards or meditating, or hitting a punching bag to be ready for sharks, or whatever mysterious and mythical things he does when he's not emerging from the mists at dawn patrol.

Someone else, some other family, will be arriving in town and checking into the cottage that was our home for the month of July. Maybe Summer will meet whoever it is. Maybe there'll be a girl my age, and maybe Summer will insist that they be summer friends, with what's left of the season. Like she did with me.

I turn away from the window, and stare at the back of the seat in front of me. Then I open my carry-on bag and remove the gift Mom found at our front doorstep while Summer and I were surfing. *Surfing*.

I can feel in my hands that it's obviously a book, wrapped in newspaper. There are words on the wrapping in black marker, written in the same hand that invited me on a postcard to ignore alien orders twenty-nine days ago. It says *Do not open before takeoff!*

That's been taken care of, so I tear the paper away. The book is revealed.

The Perfect Wave. Summer gave me her very own dog-eared and tattered copy of what she said is her favorite book. My hand goes to my heart, though Summer isn't here to see it.

On the front is a painted image of a girl riding a surfboard beneath a gigantic wave. She looks a little like Summer, but there's only one Summer.

I read the blurb on the back cover: *When the perfect wave comes, you've got to be ready to catch it.*

Of course it's incredibly cheesy, but it's also absolutely true. It's truer than anything in the books I've been reading the past year, before I met Summer. Truer than stories of zombies wanting to slurp my eyeballs, and more important than figuring out how to survive the apocalypse, which after all still hasn't happened.

I look back out the window, over my shoulder toward the sea, and suddenly I feel sure that it doesn't matter who moves into the cottage for the month of August.

The book falls open to a place held by a greeting

card, on which is a painted picture of two sets of bare feet in sand. When I open the card a photo falls out, but my eyes go first to Summer's words, written in her hand.

Juillet—
My July, my Betty.
My Bluebird.
The enclosed photo shows me in my favorite place in the universe.
Thank you for being there.
Happy Birthday—
Always, Your Summer

I pick up the photo. It's the Polaroid we had taken for five bucks. It shows Summer and me standing in front of the fountain on the promenade. It's exactly the spot where Hank got hurt.

She said that for a long time she couldn't even walk past that fountain, that it made her too sad. So why did she insist the Polaroid guy take our picture in front of it? Why would she now say it was her favorite place in the universe?

I study the picture closely. Summer is wearing her adorable blue hoodie that says *Um okay*. I'm wearing my black T-shirt with the word *DEATH*. Putting it together in my head, I realize that it was long before I even knew about Hank. It was before she told me anything about his accident at the fountain.

I look at our faces, my uncomfortable expression. I remember the feeling I held inside, that I didn't deserve to be her friend, or to even be *seen* with her. Summer is looking down in the photo, and I follow her eyes, lower, to where her open hand reaches for mine.

Then it hits me.

She brought me there to help her overcome her fear of the place.

It's just like she did for me, all over town.

Crossing Third Street. On the beach, into the shark-infested water. With practically every step.

By my side as I walked back into life.

And me, by *her* side.

My favorite place in the universe.

I slip the photo back into the card, and tuck it away in the book.

I put my hair to my nose and smell the sea.

Then I reach into my bag for a postcard and pen, and begin composing my response.

Summer—
My wildest, happiest Summer—

Acknowledgments

Thanks—

as always, to the Mighty Central Phoenix Writer's Workshop, without whom this could not have happened.

To the Beach Boys for their album *Pet Sounds*, which I listened to endlessly in the summer of its fiftieth anniversary, when this novel was born.

To the decades-old surf culture, which is impossible not to admire as an outsider. I hope I have done it justice.

To my agent, Wendy Schmalz, for everything.

To Karen Chaplin—my editor at Harper Collins—for making this book the best it could be. And to Rosemary Brosnan and everyone else at Harper—thanks for bringing three books into the world with me. We made the world a more beautiful place, no?

To my family, friends, and neighbors, for their love and support.

And to you, reader—thank you for giving me my purpose.

Dude.